THE ANGEL GIFT

DARK WORLD: THE ANGEL TRIALS 4

MICHELLE MADOW

DREAMSCAPE PUBLISHING

*T*homas and I ran through the back alleyways of Chicago with our supernatural speed, quickly arriving back at the Bettencourt.

Cassandra was waiting in his penthouse when we arrived. The bundle of the materials she'd used for the tracking spell we'd done on the demon a few hours ago was back on the dining room table. It was like she already knew what we needed.

Thomas must have reached out to her with his technopath ability—his gift that allowed him to control technology—and told her to bring the materials back here.

I was glad for it. Cassandra was the most powerful witch in this city, and we needed her help. Now.

"What's going on?" She looked back and forth

between Thomas and me in alarm. "Where are Sage and Raven?"

"They're gone." My soul felt empty as I spoke the words. "The demon we were hunting turned out to be a greater demon. He teleported away with Raven and Sage before we could stop him."

I still couldn't believe it. One second, Raven and Sage were right in front of us. I was getting ready to kill my tenth demon, which would complete the quest the Earth Angel had given to me so I could join her army in Avalon.

We'd been so close to Avalon that I could practically taste it.

Then the demon had teleported away with Raven and Sage, ripping my heart out of my chest in the process. I'd gone from excited to anguished so quickly that I could still barely process the emotions.

"We don't know where he took them," Thomas continued. "Their phones have been destroyed, so I can't locate them. We need you to do a tracking spell to find them."

Cassandra hurried to the table, laying the cloth flat and getting the items set up. "Don't both girls wear cloaking rings?" she asked.

"They do. But they're smart," I said. "They'll know to remove their rings so we can find them."

She nodded and got the necessary items into place. Four different colored candles, each representing an element and point on the compass. A pendulum with a quartz crystal. An atlas.

All tracking spells I'd observed in the past had been done with a general location in mind. This time, the atlas was opened to a map of the entire world.

Greater demons could teleport anywhere in the world.

My stomach sunk at the realization that Raven and Sage could truly be anywhere. I'd *known* it, but it was different seeing the map of the world laid out like that.

It was like the map of the world was mocking me for failing at keeping Raven safe.

I'd never been so worried in my life. Not even when I'd witnessed the Hell Gate being opened in the Vale.

I'd also never cared about someone this much in my life.

But at least I knew Raven was alive. Our imprint bond warmed my heart, steady and whole. The imprint bond would have disappeared if she'd been killed. She might not be safe—she likely wasn't—but she was alive.

Right now, that warmth over my heart was the only thing giving me hope.

I could only pray to the angels, or to the gods, or to whatever was out there, that Sage was still alive as well.

"To track them, I'm going to need an item that belonged to each of them," Cassandra said. "The closer they are emotionally to the item, the more accurate the spell will be."

"Raven and I are imprinted," I said. "Our souls are connected. Would that work?"

"It's perfect." Cassandra nodded, and then turned to Thomas. "And for Sage?" she asked. "I know it's been a few years since she stayed with us over the summers, but you must still have something here of hers that she valued."

"I do." Thomas nodded and stepped forward, wearing his constant mask of calm. "Because Sage and I are imprinted as well."

NOAH

$\mathcal{I}$ stared at Thomas in shock. "When did this happen?" I asked.

"Right before we left for the demon hunt." He cleared his throat in a rare display of discomfort. "It was when the two of us spoke alone in here. We imprinted on each other."

I knew the moment he was referring to. It was when Thomas had convinced Sage to allow him to join us on the hunt.

I figured he'd had a compelling argument to convince her. But given their history, I hadn't expected things had gone farther than talking.

I'd been wrong. Because clearly they'd kissed.

That was how shifters imprinted on each other.

Thomas and I definitely had a lot to chat about later

—such as why shifters were suddenly able to imprint on both humans *and* vampires.

But first, we needed to find our girls.

"Tell us what we need to do," I said, turning to Cassandra.

If the witch was surprised that shifters were imprinting outside our species, she did a good job at hiding it. Instead, she was focused on lighting the candles, the smells of the correlating scents filling the room.

"I can only track one thing at a time." She lit the last candle and blew out the match. "So while I hope the girls are still together, I'll need to track them both separately. I'll hold my pendulum with my right hand, and whichever one of you wants to go first will hold onto my left."

"I'm going first." Thomas walked toward Cassandra and reached for her hand. Then he glared at me. "After all, we wouldn't be in this mess if you hadn't brought Sage into it in the first place."

If I hadn't brought Sage here, she would still be in LA, hating Thomas for breaking their engagement without properly explaining why. My claws ached at the tips of my fingers, wanting to break through and fight Thomas for trying to blame me for this.

But I took a deep breath and reeled it in. I knew

better than to provoke the vampire prince now. Not when Raven's life was more and more in danger with each passing minute.

All I cared about now was saving her. So I nodded, holding the vampire's gaze. If he was surprised by my reaction, he didn't show it.

Cassandra took that as a cue to begin the spell. As she chanted the ancient words, the three of us stared at the crystal point of the pendulum, waiting for it to move.

It stayed perfectly still.

Worry creased Cassandra's brow. "Maybe it'll help if you think about her," she said to Thomas, although she sounded less confident than before.

"I *am* thinking about her," he said sharply.

The witch nodded and returned her focus to the pendulum. She stared at it, like she was trying to will it to move.

But still, nothing.

"Maybe the imprint bond isn't the best thing to use," Thomas finally said. "Sage has some things in her room. I'll go grab them."

"No." Cassandra shook her head, her eyes sad. "I know witches who have worked with shifters for the exact same thing. Locating a person they'd imprinted on. The imprint bond was the *best* thing to use. It gave the fastest, most accurate reading."

"But I'm not a shifter," Thomas said—as if any of us needed reminding. "Maybe the fact that we're different species is messing with the spell."

It sounded like he was trying to convince himself as much as he was trying to convince her.

"It's worth a try." Cassandra pursed her lips, although she didn't sound like she believed it would work. "Go find something of hers. In the meantime, I'll work with Noah to try tracking Raven."

Determination flashed in Thomas's eyes, and he zipped out of the dining room to search for something that belonged to Sage.

Finally. My turn.

I walked over to Cassandra and took her hand in mine. Her palm was clammy. I could smell the anxiety seeping from her pores. Tangy and bitter.

If we couldn't locate Raven…

I shook the thought away, not wanting to consider it. At least not yet. Just because we couldn't locate Sage, it didn't mean we wouldn't be able to locate Raven.

"Let's find her." I straightened, trying to sound as confident as possible.

As Cassandra chanted, I stared at the unmoving pendulum and thought of Raven.

I thought of the first moment I'd seen her, when she was smiling and laughing with her friends as they walked through the entrance of the Santa Monica Pier to celebrate her birthday. I thought about the first time we'd kissed, when the imprint bond had lit up my heart and dug its fingers into my soul, so deeply that I knew it would be marked forever. I thought about the ferocity in her eyes as she'd run at the demon in the alley in Nashville and killed him with the heavenly dagger. I thought about how she'd listened when I'd told her about my dark past as the First Prophet of the Vale, and how despite everything, she'd accepted me anyway.

I loved her. And I couldn't live with myself if I lost her.

The pendulum *needed* to move.

But it was still in the same spot when Thomas burst back into the room carrying an armful of Sage's clothes.

Thomas said nothing. He just stared at the still pendulum, defeat plastered across his features.

One of the shirts he was holding dropped down to his feet. He made no attempt to pick it up. "Nothing?" he asked.

"I'm sorry." Cassandra lowered her eyes and untangled her hand from mine.

Emptiness filled my chest. I didn't want to let go—it was like letting go of the chance to track Raven.

But the imprint bond was still there, warming my heart with the reminder that Raven was out there.

I couldn't let go of that.

If I did, I'd lose hope completely.

Thomas dumped the armful of Sage's clothes onto the other end of the table and pulled out a black lace top. "This was one of Sage's favorites," he said, clutching it tightly. "It still smells like her—she wore it recently. Let's see what happens when you use it to track her."

He thrust it over to Cassandra before she could reply.

I could tell from the expression in the witch's eyes that she didn't think it would work. But she nodded, and started chanting, staring at the motionless pendulum.

Nothing happened.

Eventually she gave up and placed the shirt down onto the table. "Both of the girls are cloaked," she said before we could ask any questions. "Otherwise, I would have been able to track them."

"Maybe it's because of their cloaking rings," I said. "Is there a spell to get past the spells on their rings?"

"Who made the rings?" Cassandra asked.

"Bella from the Devereux circle made Sage's," I said. "And the Voodoo Queen from New Orleans—or one of the witches in her circle—made Raven's."

"Both very powerful circles," Cassandra said, and I held my breath as I waited for her to continue.

I didn't want to jump to any conclusions. Because yes, the witches who had made the rings were powerful. But so was Cassandra.

"If their rings had been created by a low-level witch, it would be possible to gather enough magic to track them despite the spell," she continued, fingering the fabric of Sage's top as she spoke. "But with rings like those..." She shook her head, and my stomach dropped in anticipation of the bad news. Her sad eyes already said what she'd yet to speak aloud. "I'm sorry. If the rings are what's cloaking them, no witch will be able to track them."

"What do you mean by *if?*" Thomas glared at her, as if daring her to give him an answer he didn't want to hear. "They're wearing cloaking rings. Clearly that's what's cloaking them."

Cassandra swallowed nervously, although she didn't lower her gaze. "The greater demon could have brought them to a place surrounded by a barrier spell that cloaks their location. That could be what's cloaking them—not the rings. In which case, tracking them will be impossible."

"But it still could be that they haven't had a chance to

remove the rings yet," I said confidently, needing it to be true.

"It could," Cassandra said. "Especially since their captor is likely keeping a close eye on them. It's in his best interest to make sure those rings stay on their fingers."

"Sage will remove the ring the moment she has a chance," Thomas said. "I know it."

"As will Raven." The wheels in my mind were already spinning, and I turned back to Cassandra. "How much time do you need between tracking spells before burning out?"

She glanced at her watch. "If we're doing them consistently, I can manage one every half hour until sunrise," she said. "But I'll eventually crash and need sleep."

"Good," I said, since we had a few hours to go until then. "Hopefully one of them gets their ring off before sunrise."

"If given the chance, they will," Thomas said. "But we have to accept that they might not have a chance. At least not anytime soon."

"They're smart girls—they'll find a chance." I slammed my hands down on the table, not willing to accept anything else.

"Relax, wolf boy." Thomas smirked. "I agree with you. But it's unwise to put all of our eggs in one basket."

"What are you suggesting we do then?" I looked around the room, feeling trapped. I still wasn't used to tall buildings, and I hated being in them. This whole situation was only making the feeling worse. I wouldn't be able to relax until Raven was back in my arms.

"We'll have thirty minutes between each tracking spell," he said, remaining remarkably calm through all this. "During that time, we'll talk and figure out another way to pinpoint where they might be. There's an answer to every problem. And it's up to us to find it."

NOAH

Since Thomas wanted to talk, we quickly caught Cassandra up on everything that had happened before and after the greater demon had taken the girls.

"Have you ever heard of or seen a red-eyed shifter?" I asked after finishing telling how we'd offed the two of them that had attacked us in the alley. "The shade of red matches those of a demon's."

"No." She frowned. "I've never even seen a demon. I mean, I've seen drawings of them in history books, but they were banished to Hell millennia ago."

"But there has to be someone who knows something about them," I said.

"I don't know." She shrugged. "No supernatural alive has lived that long. Not even the original vampires."

I cursed, anger rushing through my veins as I thought back to the fight in the alley. "We needed one of them alive," I said.

I'd had every intention of keeping one alive.

Then the idiot had gone and thrust his neck straight through my slicer.

"It certainly would have been helpful." Thomas pressed his palm flat against the table, looking deep in thought.

"Before killing himself, the red eyed shifter told us, 'Azazel sends his regards,'" I said, needing to find *something* useful in the bit of conversation we'd had with him. "The greater demon that took Sage and Raven must be working with Azazel."

"Sage should have let me put a tracking chip in her when I asked," Thomas said. "Then we'd never be in this mess in the first place."

"When did you ask Sage to put a tracking chip in her?" I asked.

"Back when we first started dating," he said. "When she was sixteen."

"Let me guess—she rejected the idea on the spot."

"Yes," he said, which didn't surprise me in the slightest. I knew Sage. She wasn't the type of girl who'd want to be tracked. "I respected her wishes then. Now, I regret it. If she'd agreed, we'd have already found her by now."

As much as I hated to admit it, he was right. I wished Sage had accepted his offer back then, too.

Not like it would have mattered. She would have ripped out the tracking chip the moment he'd broken their engagement.

But there was no point dwelling on the past. We needed to focus on the future—a future where we found the girls.

"If you and Sage choose to mate, this won't be a problem again," I said. "Mates can communicate with each other across all distances, no matter what."

"How?" Thomas asked.

"Through our minds," I explained. Imprinting and mating were sacred to shifter culture, and we didn't share details about it with anyone. Not even other supernaturals. But since Thomas was now part of this, he deserved to understand what he was getting into. "When we're imprinted, we can only do it when we're in the same room as each other. But when we mate, we can easily communicate no matter the distance. Or so I'm told."

Possession flared in Thomas's eyes. "I'm mating with Sage the moment we find her," he said. "I'm never going to lose her again."

I didn't say anything at first. Because according to shifter tradition, he'd need the permission of Sage's alpha first. In this case, Flint. But now wasn't the time to drop that bomb on him.

"Let's focus on finding them first," I said. "You can still feel your imprint bond with Sage, right?"

"I can." He nodded.

"Which means she's still alive," I said. "And which *also* means the girls weren't taken randomly by a demon who was hunting Raven."

"How does it mean that?" Cassandra asked.

She'd been quiet for so long that I'd forgotten she was there. Now I turned to face both her and Thomas. "Because if that were the case, don't you think the demon would have killed Sage the moment he realized she wasn't what they wanted?" I asked.

Thomas said nothing. Apparently he didn't want to admit I might be right.

That was one of the things I hated most about vampires. They thought they were so much better than all other supernaturals, just because they were immortal.

"Sage is still alive," he said instead. "I feel her." He brought his hand to his chest, and I knew what he meant. He felt the warmth from the imprint bond beating in time with his heart. I felt it too, with Raven.

I was the only person alive who loved Raven and was

strong enough to have a chance to save her. Her safety was dependent on me. But that wasn't the case with Sage.

Sage had her brother—and her pack.

"We should go to Flint," I said.

"Flint asked me to *kill* you." Thomas looked at me like I'd gone crazy. "He asked me to kill Raven too. Unless you've already forgotten that fact?"

"I haven't forgotten," I said with enough warning in my tone that Thomas leaned back slightly. "But Flint's the only person who wants Sage back as much as we do. He's *desperate* to get her back. And as much as I hate it, the Montgomery pack has power. They can help us."

"Maybe." Thomas rubbed his fingers over the table, thinking. "But we can't march in there, tell Flint we lost his sister, and expect him to be calm and rational about it."

"Most definitely not." I chuckled, since calm and rational were far from the first words that popped into my mind to describe Flint Montgomery. "We also can't forget that Flint's in the process of making a shady alliance. Which is why we shouldn't go straight to the Montgomery complex. We need to go somewhere else. To someone we know we can trust."

"I take it you have an idea who that person is?" Thomas asked.

"Amber Devereux." I didn't miss a beat. "Her sister used her Final Spell to make the Devereux mansion impenetrable. The safest place we can go in LA is there."

MARA

I watched Sage stand on her toes, look up into my father Azazel's eyes, and press her lips to his.

This was part of the way Flint and I had been able to convince my father to approve our eventual mating. We'd proposed it was possible that more shifters would imprint on demons, thus joining our side.

But now, watching my father kiss Sage, something didn't feel *right*.

When Flint and I had first kissed, we'd both felt drawn to each other. His energy *pulled* me toward him, just like he'd later told me he felt pulled to me.

Our species hated each other, but kissing Flint had felt as natural as breathing.

Sage's red eyes had been blank as she'd walked

toward my father. She'd kissed him because she'd been ordered to—not because she'd wanted to. That was how the blood binding spell she and the other Montgomery pack members had participated in worked.

Once blood bound to a demon, the demon's will became your own.

Sage ended the kiss and stepped back, her eyes still empty.

I already knew what my father didn't.

"Did it work?" he asked her.

"No." Sage lowered her eyes. Her lower lip trembled—she was scared. "I'm sorry, Your Grace."

He studied her for a few seconds, his expression empty.

I held my breath, unsure what he would do. My father was normally level headed and focused. But that had changed when we'd arrived to Earth. He was feeling pressed for time, and it was making him sloppy.

"Apology accepted," he said. "You did exactly as I asked of you. It was the most you could do."

Sage beamed up at him, clearly thrilled to have not disappointed him. "We could try again, if it pleases you." She sounded as eager as ever.

Something about her tone sickened me.

"If you were going to imprint, it would have

happened already," I chimed in before he had a chance to reply.

My father glared at me, and I pressed my lips together, instantly regretting the transgression. "You'll speak only when spoken to," he said, his eyes traveling around the circle to all the members of the Montgomery pack. "That goes for all of you."

I reached for Flint's hand for support.

He didn't resist my hold. But he didn't give me the reassuring squeeze I'd grown accustomed to, either.

One glance over at him showed his eyes looked as empty as the rest of theirs.

I tried to repress the unease that crawled up my spine. But it didn't go away. It just grew stronger.

"Return to where you were standing," my father commanded Sage.

She scurried back to her spot on the other side of Flint.

He nodded once she was back in place. "It was an interesting test, but it's for the best that I didn't imprint on a shifter," he said. "I wouldn't want to do anything that might make me weak." He looked to me when he said the final part, accusation in his eyes.

I bristled, offended by what he was insinuating. Imprinting with Flint hadn't made me weak. It made me stronger.

Now that I had Flint, I had something to fight for. That was something that had been missing throughout all my centuries of life.

How had I lived for so long without ever knowing love?

But after my father's outburst, I didn't reply. I was his favorite daughter, so I didn't think he'd do anything *too* terrible to me for speaking out of turn the first time.

I couldn't count on the same for two offenses so close together.

Despite being my father, he was still a greater demon. He wasn't known for his kind punishments. And I'd worked hard to get where I was. I wasn't going to ruin that now.

My father continued to look around at the vacant red eyes of the Montgomery pack members, his lips slowly turning up into a smile. "Now that we're bonded, my will is your will," he said. "My wants are your wants. You'll have my protection until the end of time. Lavinia will lower the boundary spell now, since I know there's no longer a risk of any of you fleeing."

There were nods of approval throughout the crowd, although no one voiced their support out loud. They were simply silent, waiting for him to continue.

"Soon, we'll recruit more shifters to join our numbers," he said. "You see, shifters are special to me.

Not just to me, but to *all* of demon-kind. The first shifters were created with demon blood, just as the first Nephilim were created with angel blood. Only shifters can complete the blood binding ritual, since your blood is already connected to demon blood. But over time, the knowledge of the origin of your species has become lost. That happens over the course of a few millennia." He chuckled, as if the thousands of years we spent in Hell was no big deal. "Eventually, we'll try to convince all the shifter packs to join our cause and accept my protection. But first, there's a greater plan at play. You see, I'm in the process of acquiring something extremely important for us. Something that once we have, will make us indestructible."

I scowled. This wasn't the first time he'd mentioned this "greater plan." He'd created this plan with my Aunt Lilith and the Foster witch circle—Lavinia's circle.

They refused to let me in on it. They refused to let *anyone* in on it. I trusted my father was telling the truth that once this plan was complete, our kind would be able to defeat the creatures that lived on the Earth and have the planet for ourselves. We deserved it after surviving all those millennia trapped in Hell.

But I hated not knowing what this plan was.

"The plan is nearing completion," my father continued. "Until then, I need you to lay low. That means staying here, inside your complex, unless I require you to perform a task for me. After all, we can't have you wandering the city and having other supernaturals questioning the change of your eye colors, can we?" He looked to Flint at that last part, clearly expecting an answer.

"No, Your Grace." Flint sounded like a robot—not like the man I'd fallen in love with. "I assure you that as the alpha of the Montgomery pack, we'll stay in the complex until receiving further orders from you."

It hurt to see and hear Flint like this. He sounded like a shell of who he usually was.

But our imprint bond was still there. I could feel it.

I needed to trust our bond. The imprint bond between us was stronger than the blood bond between him and my father.

Wasn't it?

"Wonderful." My father smiled. "With that settled, it's time to move onto other matters. I know milestone celebrations are important in both in Hell and on Earth. So, tell me. What does your kind do to celebrate mating?"

My heart beat faster. Could this mean what I thought it did?

I glanced over at Flint to see his reaction. But if he was equally as excited, I couldn't tell.

He was focused purely on my father. It was like I didn't exist beside him at all.

"Once each alpha has approved the pairing, we perform a ceremony similar to a human wedding," Flint replied, his eyes only on my father's as he spoke. "The ceremony is held on the grounds of whichever mate is the dominant of the pairing, as that is the pack that the couple joins. That alpha acts as the officiate."

"And what happens if the alpha is the one joining with a mate?" my father asked.

"Then the alpha chooses who he or she would like to officiate." Despite all the clues that my father was referring to the two of us, Flint still seemed unmoved as he spoke.

Did he even want to mate with me anymore?

I felt no affection from him through the imprint bond. The imprint bond was still there, but it was weaker. Muted.

Each unemotional word he spoke was like a blow to my heart. I'd never been the most emotional person to begin with—it was natural for demons to suppress emotions, and my father raised me to believe emotions were a weakness—but this *hurt*. The pain was so physical that it hurt to breathe.

"Then you'll need to choose someone to officiate the

ceremony between you and Mara." My father smiled first at Flint and then at me, his intentions clear.

Despite the uncontrollable emotions raging through my body, I forced myself to smile back. After how hard I'd fought for my father to allow Flint and I to mate, I couldn't seem ungrateful now.

I *wasn't* ungrateful. I was getting what I wanted.

So why did it feel so wrong?

"And hopefully the ceremony won't take long to plan." If my father noticed anything amiss with how I was acting, he didn't acknowledge it as he continued, "Because I intend for the two of you to be mated by the end of the week."

he heavy metal door of the bunker slammed shut in my face.

I turned to the others in the room with me. There were about fifteen men and women of various ages, all wearing matching blue jumpsuits. The only thing different about each jumpsuit was the number on the front left of the chest.

The room had rows of bunk beds, like a hostel. It reminded me of one of the hostels I'd stayed in while backpacking around Europe.

Well, when I *thought* I'd been backpacking around Europe. That trip hadn't really happened. A witch had used memory potion to implant the memories of the Europe trip into my mind to replace something else that had happened to me. Something I suspected was terrible, although I still didn't know what it was.

One of the women in the group stepped forward. She was about my height, with light orange hair tied up in a milkmaid braid. She looked to be in her late thirties or early forties. Her jumpsuit had the number seven stitched onto it.

She gave me a small smile, and I relaxed slightly. Whoever these people were, it appeared they were on my side.

"I'm Suzanne." Her voice was as warm as her smile. "What's your name?"

I looked around again at them all suspiciously. I *wanted* to trust them.

But I'd been through hell and back since the night I'd been attacked and nearly abducted by a demon. And I'd just been dropped into this place by Azazel himself.

I didn't know if these people he'd locked me up with were humans. They could be anything—vampires, shifters, witches, demons... although I didn't think they were demons. I couldn't see through demon glamour, but I *could* see flashes of their eyes and teeth if I knew or suspected what they were. That hadn't happened since I'd been in here.

The only thing keeping me grounded right now was

the imprint bond pulsing warmly in my heart. My connection to Noah was still there and as strong as ever.

Our imprint bond would only go away if he died or if he mated with someone else. So at least I knew he was still alive.

If I didn't know that, I surely would have lost it by now.

The lady—Suzanne—slowly walked up to me and took my hands in hers.

The moment her skin touched mine, calmness rushed through me. I wouldn't say I felt suddenly safe, but I didn't feel as threatened as I had seconds earlier.

I usually wasn't one to be okay with strangers touching me. But there was something different about her. Something motherly.

"You're afraid," she said steadily, her light brown eyes focused on mine. "We all were, when we were first brought here. But we're all on the same side. We're just like you. I promise."

"You're all… gifted?" I repeated what Azazel had said back when he'd first teleported Sage and me here.

He'd said that as a demon, he could *see* the auras of humans. That gifted humans had stronger auras.

Apparently I was one of those special humans.

It certainly explained why the demons kept spotting me at every bar we visited to hunt them down.

But I didn't have a special gift. If I did, surely I'd know what it was by this point in my life.

"We are." She nodded.

"What's your gift?" I asked.

"Compassion," she answered simply. "And comfort."

I supposed that explained the motherly feeling I was experiencing from her touch. The feeling that was putting me slightly at ease and making me comfortable with the thought of opening up to her.

"My name's Raven," I finally answered her original question. "And I don't have a gift."

"I'm sure that's not true," she said.

Before I could tell her that it *was* true, the door opened again. The demon that had held me down before —Marco—stepped inside. He was tall and strong, like a bodyguard. And he was carrying a blue jumpsuit.

Suzanne dropped her hands from mine the moment he entered and stepped back to stand with the others. She nodded, as if to tell me everything was going to be okay.

But everything was *far* from okay.

"Put this on." Marco held the jumpsuit out to me. It had the number thirty-three on the front. "I'll take what you're wearing now. You won't need it anymore."

He blocked the only door that led in or out. I wasn't stupid enough to think I could get past him. Despite the self-defense techniques Noah and Sage had been teaching me the past few days, supernatural strength *always* beat human strength. It was a law of nature.

I didn't stand a chance against him.

So I took the jumpsuit and looked around the bunker. "Where do I go to change?" I asked.

He stared at me blankly. "You don't go anywhere," he said.

Realization set in. He wanted me to change right here, in front of everyone.

The others in the bunker turned to give me privacy. Since they all wore matching jumpsuits, I imagined they'd all been through the same humiliation themselves. About half of them walked back to the beds I assumed were theirs, keeping their backs to me. Only one person who remained standing peeked behind him —a guy who looked like he was at least thirty years older than me. Gross.

I stared down at the jumpsuit and took a deep breath.

"Hurry up." Marco clearly wasn't going anywhere until I did as instructed. "We don't have all day."

Best to just get this over with. Bras and panties weren't that much different than a bathing suit... right?

With that thought, I placed the jumpsuit by my feet and pulled off the shirt I was wearing—one of Sage's that she'd loaned me. It was black with gold sparkles, and the sparkles scratched my skin as I pulled it over my head and through my arms. Once off, I threw it to the floor. Then, without looking at anyone, I unbuttoned my jeans, getting out of them as quickly as possible.

The air conditioning blasted overhead, and goosebumps rose over my arms as I stood there in just my bra and underwear. Despite my earlier thought that it was no different than a bathing suit, it didn't matter. This was humiliating and degrading. Nothing I could say to myself could convince me otherwise.

I reached down for the jumpsuit, but Marco interrupted me.

"Remove your undergarments as well," he said.

I stared up at him in shock. The last shred of dignity I had left, and he was going for that, too.

"Turn around." I stared him straight in the eyes, as if daring him to say no.

"Demons care nothing for human flesh," he said simply. "Your kind doesn't incite desire in ours."

"I don't care." I clenched my jaw, wishing I were strong enough to punch the smug look off his face. "I'm not changing in front of you. Turn around. Now."

He kept his eyes locked on mine. He was trying to intimidate me. But I wouldn't let him do that. So I did what I'd witnessed the Montgomery wolves doing when I'd been in their complex—I held his stare.

My dignity was all I had left. I wouldn't let him take it from me too.

Turn around, I thought, continuing to hold his gaze. I breathed steadily, listening to each breath as it went in and out. I refused to budge. I might not be able to physically fight this demon, but I could handle a battle of wills.

Noah had always told me I was the most stubborn person he knew.

After what felt like an entire minute of silent staring had passed, Marco scowled and turned to face the door.

I said nothing, instead stripping out of my bra and underpants as quickly as possible and hurrying to put on the jumpsuit. There was underwear built in, and it had a zipper in front. I did the zipper up.

Marco turned back around once the zipper clicked in place. The others all turned around as well.

My cheeks were heated, surely a bright shade of red. I focused on my feet. I couldn't look any of them in the eyes.

They'd likely all gone through the same thing, but I had no interest in acknowledging that at the moment.

So I kneeled down to where I'd tossed my clothes to the ground and gathered them into a pile. I purposefully hid my undergarments between the shirt and pants. Then I held out the bundle for Marco to take.

He took them. But he still stared at me, looking unsatisfied.

"Jewelry too," he said.

I instinctively reached for my crystal necklace, my heart dropping. It was the only thing I had that connected me to my mom.

"Now, or I'll rip it off you myself," he growled. "The doctor wants you in the best condition possible, but if you don't give me a choice..." He smiled, his pointed yellow demon teeth flashing under the glamour of his perfect pearly whites. "I'll be sure to make it hurt."

The necklace is only a thing, I reminded myself. Yes, it made me feel connected to my mom. But she'd want me to remain safe more than anything else. And my ring... well, it was a cloaking ring. I should have thought to take it off by now anyway.

With it off, Noah could track me and find me.

I removed both the necklace and the ring, placing them on top of the pile of clothes in Marco's arms.

"A cloaking ring." He raised his eyebrow when I placed the ring down.

I didn't confirm or deny it. I just stood still, saying nothing.

"You won't be needing that here, anyway," he continued. "We have a circle of powerful witches on our side. They've placed a spell around the bunker to keep anyone from tracking you."

My heart dropped. So much for that plan.

He had me scan my thumb onto his phone to get me "set up in the system," and then he turned around to leave me with the others once more.

I narrowed my eyes as I watched him leave. I felt so cold and alone. The demons had taken everything from me.

Except that wasn't true. The imprint bond warming my heart reminded me that I had Noah. And somewhere out there, I had my mom. Wherever she was, I was going to save her.

Which meant I needed to fight back and get out of here.

I wasn't sure how.

But I wouldn't give up until trying everything.

RAVEN

*T*he sound of the door slamming shut echoed through the room, punctuated with silence.

I turned around, forcing myself to face the others. Not all of them met my eyes. The ones who did all watched me with pity.

I felt so humiliated. Weak. Victimized.

That was the last way I wanted to feel, but feelings were rarely something one could control.

"Was it the same for all of you?" I asked, my voice soft.

"It was," Suzanne said. She, of course, was the first to walk forward, although she didn't reach for me again.

I was glad for it. After what had just happened, I felt violated and disgusting. The *last* thing I wanted was to be touched.

"I know it's not much, but all of us are here for you," she said, giving me a small smile. "Which do you prefer —a top or bottom bunk?"

I looked at the beds lined up along the walls, and at that moment, it hit me for real. Until I could brainstorm a way out, I was stuck here. The doors in the bunker could only be opened with fingerprint identification. They were solid metal, too strong to break down.

Was there ever another time in my life when I'd felt so trapped? No. Nothing compared to this. The most trapped I'd felt until now was while working the cash register at my mom's new age shop, Tarotology.

I'd hated working there.

Now, I'd give anything to go back there. It was funny, wishing for what I once hated. I guess it was true that you never knew what you had until it was gone.

"Top," I made a split second decision. Being in a bottom bunk would surely make me feel more trapped than I already did.

"Perfect," Suzanne said. "There's an empty top bunk above mine."

She motioned for me to follow her to the other side of the room, and I did. A few people glanced at me when I walked by. Most ignored me.

Once we reached her bunk, she placed her hand on the bed that would be mine. "Here we are," she said with a warm smile. "I know this is hard, Raven. But I want to make this transition as easy for you as I can. Okay?"

"Do you do this for everyone?" I looked around at the others in the room. Some were watching me curiously, and others had books in front of them, reading. The ones who were watching me looked away the moment my eyes met theirs.

"I do." She chuckled, although her eyes were sad. "I suppose I've taken on the role of camp counselor. You see, we've all been in the same position as you right now. We know how important it is not to bombard you. You'll get to know everyone soon. But to get you situated, I'll tell you how things work around here, give you the grand tour, and answer any questions you have. Sound good?"

"Sure," I said, since I planned on getting out of here. The best start would be to ask as many questions as I could. I'd arm myself with information. That's what Noah and Sage did before their hunts. The more information I had, the better chance I had at success. "How long have you been here?" I asked.

"Forty-six days," she replied.

"And in all that time, you didn't try to escape?"

"There is no escape." She shook her head sadly. "The only way out of here is to do well enough on your physical and health assessments to be moved to the next location."

"Where's that?" I perked up, hope filling my chest at the thought that there might be an actual way out.

"I don't know." Suzanne shrugged. "None of us do. And they won't tell you, so I don't recommend asking. It just makes them angry."

"The demons?" I asked.

"And the doctor."

I didn't have time to ask about the doctor before lights in the corners of the ceiling started flashing overhead. It was like a fire warning.

"What's going on?" I looked around in alarm. None of the others looked panicked. But they started shuffling around in their bunks—putting their books away and heading toward the door.

"Dinner time," Suzanne answered. "Do you like boiled meat, rice, and vegetables?"

"Sort of?" It certainly wasn't my preferred meal of choice, but I wasn't opposed to those things.

"Good, because you're going to be getting a lot of them." She headed toward the door and motioned for me to follow. "Come on. The first stop on our tour is the dining hall."

*T*homas unblocked the service on my phone to allow me to call Amber. He controlled whose phones worked or not in the Bettencourt with his technopath ability. I took his allowance to let mine work as an admission that the two of us *might* be becoming friends.

Amber was quick to agree to let our gang stay with her and her circle in the Devereux mansion. It turned out she knew Cassandra—the two of them were distant cousins. That helped a ton with getting her to trust Thomas as well.

My stuff was already packed and ready to go, and it didn't take long for Thomas and Cassandra to gather theirs. Once ready, we gathered in the living room to head out.

We'd be traveling the quickest way possible—teleportation. But Cassandra could only teleport one person at a time. That was typical for witches, and for most creatures that could teleport. The fact that the greater demon that had taken Raven and Sage had been able to take them both at once demonstrated how majorly powerful he was.

Going against him was *not* going to be easy.

But that hadn't stopped me in the past, and I certainly wasn't going to let it stop me now.

Cassandra had never been to the Devereux mansion before, which meant it was going to be harder for her to accurately teleport us there. But Thomas was able to zoom in on the house's location using satellite map view, and Amber showed her what the interior of the house looked like through video chat.

Once Cassandra was confident about the location, she teleported me there first. We figured it was best to bring me first instead of Thomas since I'd met Amber and her circle before.

My stomach swooped as the world disappeared around me, and I instinctively closed my eyes as we made our way through the ether. I didn't know where we went in the seconds between leaving a place and arriving at the intended destination, but my instinct had always been to close my eyes.

My feet hit the ground, and I opened my eyes to find myself standing in the middle of the Devereux living room.

Amber waited for us on the couch. She wore a bright pink jumpsuit and was swirling a matching pink martini in her hand. Her blonde hair was pulled up into a high ponytail, like she'd just finished working out.

She would have looked like a typical Beverly Hills housewife who didn't have a care in the world, but the dark circles under her eyes said otherwise.

The three other members of her circle sat on the couch perpendicular to hers. They all had pink drinks in their hands as well, and their dark magic smelled like maple syrup that had been sitting out for too long. Together, their magic smelled so strong that it practically blocked out Amber's light magic floral scent.

Amber had always been the one to work with customers who dropped by for spells and potions. The others stayed in the background. The fact that they were here showed that a lot had changed since the last time Sage and I had been here.

It was understandable, given that Azazel had murdered their fifth circle member. They hated him as much as I did.

Which was exactly why I trusted them.

"Perfect landing." Amber regarded Cassandra with a

closed-lip smile and took a sip of her martini. "Powerful magic clearly runs in the family."

"Of course it does." Cassandra returned her smile and looked each of the witches in the eyes. "Let me grab Thomas, and then we can get better acquainted."

She flashed out, leaving me alone with the four witches.

I shuffled my feet and looked around the lofty living room, unsure what to do.

"Would you care for a drink?" asked one of the witches whose name I didn't know. She wore all black, had inky hair that fell all the way down to her back, and eyes rimmed with kohl. It was like she wanted the world to know that her magic was dark, and that she was proud of it.

"Sure." I glanced questionably at the pink martini in her hand. I wasn't one for girly drinks, but at the same time, I didn't want to insult their hospitality.

"Don't worry—we have other options," she said. "How about a beer?"

"That's perfect."

She seemed pretty chill—like the type of girl Sage would get along with. She returned with my beer just as Cassandra flashed into the living room with Thomas.

He glanced around the mansion's modern interior

with clear approval. Then he walked to stand in the front of the room, facing the witches.

"Thank you for hosting us," he said. "I'm Thomas Bettencourt, leader of the Bettencourt vampire coven of Chicago. I assume Amber has already told you why we're here?"

"She has," the witch in the all-black getup who'd gotten me my beer said. "I'm Bella. You've already met Amber over the phone. Our other two sisters are Evangeline and Doreen." She looked at each of them as she spoke their names. They both wore casual jeans and t-shirts, and had similarly colored brown hair. I doubted I'd be able to remember which of the two witches was which. "Do you and Cassandra want drinks? Noah struck me as more of a beer guy, but I'm getting a cabernet vibe from you..."

"Intuitive." Thomas nodded in approval. "Cassandra and I will have a bottle of your finest cabernet."

Bella got them situated with their drinks, and the group of us settled on the couch. To an outsider, we might have looked like old friends reuniting. But the tension in the room was thick with questions—and worry about whatever was to come.

I sipped my beer, but the chilled drink did nothing to soothe my nerves.

They wouldn't be soothed until Raven was back in my arms where she belonged.

"I'm guessing Amber told you why we're here?" I jumped on starting the conversation before Thomas had the chance.

"She did," one of the other witches—either Evangeline or Doreen—said. "Ever since the passing of our sister Whitney, the Devereux circle is dedicated to assisting supernaturals in whatever they need to fight against the demons."

"Ever since Azazel *murdered* our sister Whitney," Bella corrected her, her eyes hard.

Amber blinked away tears and took a large swig of her pink drink. "Whitney used her Final Spell to create a powerful barrier around our mansion. It's now the safest place in LA," she said. "It might even be the safest place in the country. We refuse to let her sacrifice be in vain. So whatever you need, we'll do everything we can to help."

"Have you coordinated with the Earth Angel on Avalon?" Thomas asked.

"Avalon is impossible to track down—we suspect it might exist on a different plane entirely," Amber said. "We've tried to get word to her that we want to help, but we haven't been able to reach her."

She was trying to hide it, but I could see the worry in

her eyes.

I got it. It *was* worrisome that the Earth Angel hadn't communicated with anyone on Earth since going to Avalon months ago. But I'd met her. Annika was determined to use her powers to bring together an army strong enough to vanquish the demons that had escaped the Hell Gate. Plus, she had the angels on her side.

She and her army were our only chance at winning this war.

"Once Raven and Sage are back, we're heading to Avalon," I said. "One of the first things I'll do when I get there is tell the Earth Angel to get in touch with you."

"Thank you." Amber smiled.

"It's the least I can do," I said. "But first, we need to get to Raven and Sage. Do you have ways of tracking people other that the typical tracking spell?" I focused on Bella, since she seemed the most powerful of the three dark witches. "Ways that use dark magic?"

"Tracking spells can only be done with light magic," Bella said. "If Cassandra couldn't locate your friends with her spell, they can't be found that way."

Any hope I'd had that the dark witches could do something to track Raven and Sage deflated in a second. But I wouldn't be defeated so easily. We *could* save the girls. I wouldn't rest until we did.

"Flint doesn't know Sage is missing yet, but once he

does, he'll be out to find her just as much as we are." I leaned forward, fire rushing through my veins at the prospect of taking action. "Pack always helps pack. The entire Montgomery pack will join us, and they have the numbers to help us find and rescue Raven and Sage from the greater demon that took them. We need to go to the compound and talk to him as soon as possible."

"Except that Flint put a bounty on Noah's head." Thomas sighed and took a sip of his wine. "He's making it sound far easier than it will be."

"The group of us together is just as strong as the Montgomery pack—perhaps even stronger," I said. "If we all go there, the pack won't fight us. Especially once they hear what we have to say."

Amber looked around at her sisters in alarm. "My sisters and I can't leave the house at the same time," she said. "We need at least two of us here at all times to keep watch."

"I thought this mansion was the safest place in LA?" I asked.

"It is," she said. "But the boundary spell is strongest when there are at least two of us here to add magical fuel to it. One light, and one dark. And we don't know what the demons are capable of. We can't let our guards down. Not even for a second."

"Bursting into the Montgomery complex was never a

good idea anyway," Thomas brushed away my idea like it was nothing. "Flint is in the midst of making a powerful alliance, so there could easily be more than just his pack there when we showed up. They might not want to help us."

"If they're allied with the Montgomerys, it means they're on their side," I said. "Sage—one of their pack members and their alpha's *sister*—was just taken by a greater demon. Of course they'll want to help us."

"You're letting your emotions for Raven and Sage get in the way of logic," Thomas said. "When I spoke with Flint, he sounded desperate. Desperate people make imprudent alliances. The Montgomery pack might want to help us, but their alliance might not. We'd be foolish to deliver ourselves to their doorstep like pigs to the slaughterhouse. We can't save our girls if we're dead."

I glared at him and took a swig of my beer, hating that he had a point. Not having Raven by my side was making me irritable in a way I'd never been before. But if I wanted to approach this correctly, I needed to rein in my emotions.

I needed to think clearly enough to save her.

"Fine," I said, still hating that he was right. "What do you think we should do then?"

"We need to spy on them first," he said simply. "That

way we can see what they're up to and plan the best way to approach them."

"It's not a terrible idea," one of the Devereux witches —either Evangeline or Doreen—said.

"But the Montgomery complex is well protected," Amber chimed in. "I put the spell on it myself."

"What spell?" I knew enough about witches to know it couldn't be a boundary spell. To maintain a boundary spell, a witch had to be living inside the compound. When I'd stayed in the Montgomery pool house, only wolf shifters lived there.

"A detection spell," she said. "To alert them whenever a non-pack member steps onto their property."

Thomas rubbed his chin in thought. "That's nothing a bit of technology can't handle," he said, an excited gleam in his eye. He looked to me and asked, "Can you put aside your wolf instincts to burst in there and fight, and instead work with me on approaching this logically?"

As a vampire prince, Thomas was higher up on the supernatural totem pole than I was. So I appreciated his including me in the decision process instead of taking charge himself.

"How long will it take?" I couldn't handle sitting around waiting much longer. He was right about the "wolf instinct" thing. A huge part of me wanted to shift into wolf form, run into the mountains, and hunt to work off all my anxious energy. But I fought against it.

Any time spent not trying to save Raven wasn't worth spending at all.

"I can have the equipment delivered within twenty-four hours," he said. "From there it'll take a bit of tinkering—and some spells and potions from the witches—and we'll be ready to go." He glanced over at the witches, as if making sure this was okay with them.

"Our house is your house." Bella's red lips curled into a smile. "You've got both light and dark witches at your disposal here. So whatever spells and potions you need, you'll get."

"Then let's get that equipment here," I said. "And let's save our girls."

RAVEN

*E*veryone filed out of the bunk, through the hall, and into the dining area. Suzanne walked beside me the whole way.

The dining room was sparsely decorated. It was just clusters of circular tables, like a high school cafeteria. But unlike a high school cafeteria, plates of food were already set down at each spot.

Some of the plates had more food on them than others, but the portions were all substantial. There were little place cards next to each plate, each one with a number on it.

It was something you'd expect to see at a formal meal —not for humans being kept prisoners by demons. And the demons weren't letting us forget that we were their captives. There were four of them in the dining hall, including Marco. All of them were men. Each stood guard, keeping his eyes on us.

"We all have to sit at our numbered seat," Suzanne said, glancing at the thirty-three on my jumpsuit. "I'll help you find yours."

She walked me to a table on the far end of the room, where five others were already getting situated. I felt silly being escorted by Suzanne. But in such unfamiliar territory, it was nice having a friend to take care of me.

Especially because while Suzanne looked nothing like my mother, her personality reminded me of her.

There was, of course, a chance that she was a spy for the demons. But my gut told me she wasn't. Her gift of compassion was genuine. I'd felt it when she'd touched me earlier. And she truly seemed to care about teaching me about life here.

Not like I intended on staying here. But I was grateful for her help just the same.

I approached the table looked at the place cards. Numbers thirty-one through thirty-six. Suzanne's jumpsuit was number seven. It didn't take a genius to figure out she wouldn't be sitting with us.

I placed my hand on the back of the chair for number thirty-three and stared down at the colorless food on my plate. Boiled chicken, steamed rice, and vegetables.

It looked blander than the tofu and quinoa my mom occasionally cooked us for dinner.

"Be sure to finish everything on your plate." Suzanne patted my arm encouragingly. "I'll come back once the meal is over and give you the tour of the bunker. It isn't big, so you'll see everything before lights out."

"You take this camp counselor thing seriously, don't you?" This whole situation was so ridiculous that I couldn't help trying to make a joke of it.

"You bet." She flashed me a smile and hurried over to her table on the other side of the room.

Marco had his eye on us the entire time, and he continued to watch me once Suzanne walked away. If I tried to make a run for it, he'd be on me in a second. Plus, where would I go? Any door that led out of here was locked.

I also couldn't ignore the gnawing hunger in my stomach. It had been forever since I'd last eaten, and I was starting to feel light-headed because of it. That always happened to me when I hadn't eaten in a few hours. My mom used to joke that I was impossible to be around when I was hangry. I never refuted it, since I knew she was right.

"You might as well sit down," one of my tablemates— a girl who looked a few years younger than me—said. Her hair was dyed black, although she had blonde roots growing out at the top. "Better to do it yourself than have one of the demons force you."

I didn't disagree with her, so I pulled out the chair and took a seat. Marco's stance relaxed slightly when I did. He still watched me, but he was one of those people who managed to watch everyone in the room while still making you feel like he was only looking at you.

I turned away from him and focused on my tablemates instead. "I'm Raven." I looked at the teen girl when I introduced myself, since she'd said something to me first.

"Jessica," she said, and the others quickly followed suit in telling me their names. Craig, Valerie, Harry, and Pam.

I repeated their names in my mind a few times so I wouldn't forget.

If I was going to arm myself with information, I needed to befriend as many people as possible so I could *learn* that information. This seemed like a good place to start.

"How long have you been here?" I asked, flashing them my best *we're just out to eat and not imprisoned by demons* smile.

Luckily, they were quick to open up to me. Other than myself, Pam had been here the shortest—only for two weeks. Harry was the oldest of us all, and he'd been here for nearly three months.

I couldn't imagine being down here that long. How was he not going stir-crazy?

"If only my wife could see me now." He patted his stomach and chuckled. "She always wanted me to get rid of my beer belly. Three months of exercise and this tasteless food has certainly done that for me."

He had a slight beer belly, but nothing so extreme that I would have noticed if he hadn't said anything.

"They let you exercise?" I asked.

"More like *make*." Jessica rolled her eyes, waving her fork around in the air as she spoke. "I always hated gym at school. If only my classmates could see me now. Now I could be a track star."

"You almost make it sound like the demons care about our health," I said as I cut into the chicken. I took a bite, and discovered it tasted as bland as it looked.

I supposed it would have been too much to ask the demons to bring some salt and pepper to the table.

"They do," Pam said. "That's the only way to get to the next location. Get fit and healthy enough, and they'll send you on your way."

"From the looks of you, you're practically there already," Craig said. "It shouldn't take you long to strengthen up and move on."

I wrapped an arm around my stomach. Something about this felt *wrong*. But I needed to keep asking questions. It was the only way to learn more.

"Do any of you know where the next location is?" I figured it couldn't hurt to ask, even though Suzanne had told me not to.

"Nope," Valerie said. "But it's better than here."

"How do you know that?"

"Because that's what they tell us." She looked nervously off to the side, where one of the demons stood guard.

The demons were totally listening to our conversation. But they must not have cared, because they did nothing to silence us.

Which meant this was what they *wanted* us to think.

Which instantly made me suspect it wasn't true.

"You believe them?" I lowered my voice, even though the demons could still listen in with their supernatural hearing.

"I want to get out of here." She scooped a pile of rice onto her fork, her eyes hard. "If getting fit and becoming a member of the clean plate club is the way to do it, then that's what I'll do." She shoved all the rice into her mouth, as if to accentuate her point.

"They really make you eat everything on your plate?" I cut up some of the chicken and mixed it in with the rice, hoping that would make it taste better. It did, but only slightly.

"Yep," Jessica said. "We're not allowed to leave the dining hall until everyone's plate is clean. Bunker rules."

"Bunker rules?" I raised an eyebrow. "Or demon rules?"

"Doctor rules, technically." Pam glanced over at a middle-aged, bald man sitting at a table by himself. He was hunched over as he ate, completely focused on his food. It was like he was pretending the rest of us didn't exist. "That's him," she said. "You'll meet him tomorrow for your first examination. He calculates what size portions we all get, and we have to eat every bite of it at every meal. No exceptions."

"What if someone has an allergy?" I asked. "Or if they're vegan?"

Of course, I was thinking about my mom when I asked that last question. She wouldn't eat an animal product even if someone tried to shove it down her throat.

"Allergies are worked around," Harry said. "Not vegans." He paused and smiled, like he was remembering something. "It's funny you asked, because we used to have a vegan here. She made a big fuss about the meat at dinner the first night. But by the end of the meal she'd eaten every last bite of her chicken, just like the rest of us. It was for the best, if you ask me. Humans are supposed to eat meat. We don't have these sharp teeth for nothing." He opened his mouth and pointed at his incisors, as if I was unaware of what human teeth looked like.

"You would hate my mom," I said as I picked around at my food. A few bites of this bland meal had been enough to curb my hunger. It was going to take a lot of will power to force myself to finish it all. "She hasn't had a bite of animal product since she was twelve."

"Just like Skylar." Valerie shook her head in clear disapproval. "But that changed once she got here. There's nothing like threats from a demon to get you to do something you never imagined you'd do."

"What?" I dropped my fork and stared at Valerie, cold shock running through my body.

"The demons get to everyone." She skittishly glanced around at the ones in the room. "They out number us, out power us—"

"I know that," I cut her off. "But the vegan who was here. Skylar." I could barely say her name without a lump forming in my throat.

"What about her?" Valerie picked up what was left of her chicken and gnawed at the bone. She looked more interested in it than in talking to me.

"You knew her?" It took all my control to stop myself

from knocking that bone out of Valerie's hands so she'd pay attention to me.

"She's moved onto the next location." She shrugged, putting down the bone and starting on her veggies. "What's it to you?"

"It's everything to me," I said. "Because Skylar Danvers is my mother."

RAVEN

*V*alerie finally looked up at me, her eyes wide. "How did I not see it immediately?" she said, mystified. "The hair, the eyes, the nose. You're a splitting image of her."

My heart beat with excitement, and my stomach dropped with dread.

This was huge. It was a lead about where Azazel had brought my mom after taking her from our apartment.

But it also meant that my mom had been here, in this depressing prison bunker. And if she'd been taken to the next location...

I hoped my instinct was wrong, and that the next location wasn't worse than this place.

If people were brought to the next location once they were deemed fit and healthy enough, I wasn't surprised my mom had already been taken there. Along with being vegan, she was also a fitness nut.

A strong body creates a strong mind and soul, she'd always said.

I'd never listened, which I'd regretted once I'd started training with Noah and Sage. Their training sessions beat me into a red, huffing, sweaty mess.

"Did you know her?" I asked Valerie.

"I did." She nodded. "We all did. She had the same number as you. Thirty-three. She had every meal with us while she was here."

"Not that she was here for long," Harry added. "She was moved to the next location a few days ago."

I sucked in a sharp breath, frozen in place. I'd missed my mom by a few *days*. I couldn't believe my bad luck.

Maybe I should have been comforted by the fact that my mom had recently been in the same place I was sitting now. But I felt more alone than ever.

It felt like the universe, the gods, the angels, or *whatever* was out there was stacked against me. How was I supposed to come out victorious with so many odds not in my favor?

I had no idea. All I knew was that my mom was in the next location.

Which meant I needed to get there.

But if the next location was anything like this—or if

it was worse—what chance did my mom and I have of getting out? I wanted to *save* her, not get trapped with her.

To do that, I needed a plan.

I wasn't sure what plan that was yet. But I'd figure it out. I just needed to keep doing my research. Keep trying to figure out where the next location was, and learn as much as I could about the others trapped in this bunker with me.

It wasn't much, but it was enough to keep me from going crazy. Hopefully.

"Your mom was great," Jessica said softly. "She said her gift was reading the tarot. She didn't have any tarot cards here, but she did palm readings for all of us for fun."

"Were her readings accurate?" I asked, leaning forward slightly. I loved hearing about my mom. It made me feel close to her, even though she wasn't here with me now.

"They were positive and hopeful." Jessica shrugged. "But she wasn't telling us what she really saw."

"How do you know?"

"I can tell when people are lying," she said simply, finishing off the final piece of asparagus from her plate. "It's my gift."

I nodded, making a mental note to never lie to

Jessica. Not like I was the type of person to go around lying to people. But still. It was good to know.

"You all know what your gifts are?" I asked, looking around at the four others at the table.

They did, and they went around the circle answering my question.

Harry had perfect aim with weapons. He was a champion gun shooter, apparently one of the best in the country.

Pam wasn't sure what hers was, but she thought it was a natural sense of time. She didn't need a watch. She just instinctively always knew what time it was.

Craig could drink all the alcohol he wanted without getting drunk. This had deemed him the title of "beer pong king" in his fraternity. Pills had no effect on him, either. I asked if witch potion affected him, but he'd never tried it, so he didn't know.

Valerie could sense ghosts. Hers creeped me out the most. It was no wonder she had a sour look on her face all the time. I would, if I were constantly aware of ghosts, too.

As they each told me their gifts, I mentally cataloged which ones might be useful in getting out of here.

"Jessica." I looked back at her, since hers interested me the most. "Have you been able to tell if the demons are lying about the next location?"

She glanced around nervously, and then focused back on me. "They're not lying about its existence," she said, tapping her fingers against the top of the table. "The next location is definitely somewhere they bring us after we're given clearance by the doctor."

"Is it a good place or a bad place?" I asked.

"They won't say." She shrugged. "They knew about my gift when they brought me here, so they've been very careful about what they say around me."

I couldn't help but suspect that this was a bad sign. If the next location was better than this, surely they'd say it to Jessica so she could verify they were telling the truth.

Now I feared for my mom's safety more than ever.

But I had to keep reminding myself about what Rosella had said when Noah and I had spoken with her on the Pier. I could save my mom by going to Avalon and completing the Angel Trials.

Since I wasn't at Avalon yet, that meant my mom was alive. And worrying about her wasn't doing me any good right now. I needed to stay focused. I was already learning a lot about the others in this bunker with me. I needed to keep doing what I was doing.

"What about you?" I asked, turning to Harry. "Has your gift been... useful here?" I didn't want to speak too loudly, knowing the demons were listening.

Sure enough, when I glanced at Marco, his eyes were trained at our table.

"Nope." Harry speared a vegetable with his fork. "I'll tell you more later."

Code that he didn't want to talk about it when the demons were hovering over us.

I nodded in understanding and moved onto Valerie. Her gift with ghosts freaked me out, but there were certainly ways it might be useful.

Her haunted eyes focused on her nearly empty plate. At least now I understood *why* she looked so haunted.

"How does your gift work?" I asked softly. Given how traumatized she looked, I didn't want to intrude. But at the same time, I did, since intruding could help get us out of here. "Can you actually talk to ghosts?"

"No." Her eyes were wide and sharp as she looked at me. Freaky. "I can sense them. Whenever there's one near, chills run through my body. Like this." She held up her arm, and sure enough, goosebumps ran across her flesh.

"A ghost is here now?" I set my fork down and looked around. I'd never believed in ghosts, but now that Valerie was claiming they were real...

It was seriously creepy. I had an instinctual disdain toward things I couldn't see or hear, and I was *not* thrilled with the possibility that ghosts could be anywhere at anytime.

"Two of them," she said. "They stay in this bunker with us. Like all ghosts, they're angry. It's why they haven't passed on to the Beyond."

"How do you know this if you can't talk to them?" I asked.

"I can sense their feelings," she said. "I hate it. When I got here, I asked if the demons or the doctor knew how to get rid of our gifts. They don't. I'll be stuck sensing angry ghosts until the day I die."

I didn't know what to say—sorry hardly seemed like enough. "I can't imagine what that must be like," I eventually said, even though it wasn't totally the truth. Because I *could* imagine what it would be like. It would be awful. And I was glad I'd never know.

Jessica gave me a knowing look. She knew I was lying.

"What's your gift?" Pam—the one who could sense time—asked me. Her accent made it obvious she was from the Deep South. "We told you ours. It's only fair you tell us yours."

"I don't know." I lowered my eyes, using my fork to play with the food remaining on my plate.

"You can't not know," Valerie said. "We're different

from regular people. We've known it our whole lives. All of us."

"I'm literally the world's biggest skeptic," I told her. "I didn't even believe my mom could truly read tarot until I was thrown into the supernatural world earlier this month. I thought it was a hoax. Now the demons say I'm gifted but..." I trailed, shrugging in defeat. "I have no idea what my gift might be."

The four others at the table all looked to Jessica. Clearly, they were checking to see if they should believe me or not.

"She's telling the truth," Jessica confirmed.

I gave her a grateful smile. I had a feeling her gift would come in handy.

"Does everyone here know what their gift is?" I asked, looking around the cafeteria. There were seven tables of six, so forty-two of us in all.

"Most of them have known forever," Harry said, and I looked back at him, focusing on forcing down the bland boiled chicken as he spoke. "Not me. I mean, I always knew I had a talent with guns—with any item I could throw, really. But I figured it was a natural skill. Something I was good at and worked hard to perfect. I never thought there was anything supernatural involved. Finding out kinda took my pride away about what I can do, to be honest."

"No one should ever be too proud," Pam said. "But it's still something you can do, gifted to you by God himself. There's no need to be ashamed about that."

"I guess." He shrugged. "But once I get out of here, I don't imagine competing will be much fun anymore. Knowing my aim is some kind of supernatural 'gift' doesn't make it seem fair."

"Be grateful you have something useful." Valerie pursed her lips, staring him down. "And that you're not stuck sensing angry ghosts. Trust me when I say it isn't pleasant."

That shut him up, since it *was* a good point. We were all silent for a few seconds afterward.

"Now, about your gift," Pam broke the silence. She clasped her hands in front of her empty plate—she was one fast eater—and focused on me. "I bet you know deep down what it is, even if you don't think you do yet."

"I don't," I said. "I honestly have no idea what it is."

"Well, do you mind if we ask you some questions?" she asked, all southern sweetness. If she were from LA, I would have thought she was being fake. But she seemed too genuine to even *think* about being fake. "I bet we'll be able to figure out by lights out tonight. Well, this morning. Ten AM, to be exact. They keep us on a nocturnal schedule down here."

Since our watches and phones had been taken away, maybe her sense of time wasn't so useless, after all.

"Go ahead," I said, since I had nothing to lose. "I meant it when I said I was clueless, but I suppose it's worth a try."

RAVEN

I didn't get any closer to figuring out my gift during dinner. The others asked me tons of questions, but nothing led us anywhere. They were just as baffled as I was.

At the end of the meal, the demons checked to make sure everyone had cleaned their plate and drank all their water. I'd done as I was supposed to do and eaten everything. Firstly, because I was hungry. The food was bland, but at least it was food. And secondly, because rebelling against the demons at this point wouldn't do me any good.

I didn't know what sort of punishments the demons inflicted against those who broke the rules. But dealing with a punishment right now would only make it more difficult to escape later.

People who instantly reacted got attention in the moment. Long-term thinkers got what they wanted in the end. That was something I'd always reminded myself back in school, whenever I turned down invitations from friends to go out and party because I needed to stay in and study instead.

Yes, escaping a prison run by demons was going to be harder than getting to the end of the semester with a perfect GPA. But one of my favorite movie quotes said, "If you put your mind to it, you can accomplish anything."

I was determined to get out of this place, so that was what I was putting my mind to.

Suzanne found me once we were dismissed from dinner and gave me the tour of the bunker, as she'd promised. We could only access four areas—the sleeping quarters, dining room, gym, and bathroom. Each door had a fingerprint reader, and was programmed to only allow us to enter during certain times of the day.

As she gave me the tour, I imagined my mom everywhere. It was crazy to think she was here a few days ago.

I missed her so badly it hurt.

The bathroom and sleeping quarters were the only rooms we could access at all hours. (The bathroom was co-ed, which was definitely going to take some getting used to.) We were only allowed inside the dining hall during the three mealtimes, and were always escorted there by the demons. The gym was open between lights on and lights out. We were required to go to the gym once a day. Apparently I'd be getting a strict exercise regime from the doctor after my assessment with him tomorrow.

I *never* went to the gym at home. Therefore, most of the equipment inside of it looked foreign to me. I might as well have stepped onto an alien spaceship for all I'd known.

Hopefully this strict exercise regime came with detailed instructions, or I was going to be seriously lost. And I definitely planned on doing the exercises. Getting in shape fit in with my long-term plan.

I'd be more likely to get out of here—and more likely to pass the Angel Trials once I got to Avalon—if I was in better shape.

Plus, Noah and Sage would be disappointed if I slacked on my training.

When we returned to the sleeping quarters I found a basket of basic toiletries, a bath towel, and a fresh jumpsuit with the number thirty-three laid out on my bed. The towel wasn't plush by any means, but it would do.

Suzanne had a nearly identical pile waiting for her, although her jumpsuit had her number seven, and she didn't have a basket since she already had one stowed under our bunk.

"The demons always have a fresh jumpsuit and towel ready for us after dinner," she explained.

"That's nice of them." I reached over and ran my fingers along the jumpsuit. "Why do they care if our clothes—and bodies—are clean?"

"They don't want us to smell," Suzanne said with a small laugh. "Along with going to the gym, we're also required to shower and change into clean clothes each day. We suspect it's because stinky humans bother their heightened sense of smell."

I couldn't help but chuckle at the ridiculousness of all of this. "I haven't seen many demons around—only four or five, at the most," I said. "How do they make sure we're all exercising—and showering—each day?"

"There are cameras everywhere." She glanced up at what I'd thought was a fire sprinkler in the ceiling. "They watch everything we do."

One more piece of knowledge to add to my growing list of things I'd learned here.

As it was, I was happy to have a shower. It had been a long day, and I wanted to wash the ick off my body that I still felt from having the demon watch me change.

There were "fire sprinklers" in the bathroom as well, so the demons were watching us in there too. But it was different than being forced to strip down in a room full of clothed strangers.

The bathroom was similar to those in college dorms, with rows of showers, toilet stalls, and sinks. I had to scan my fingerprint to get the water to turn on. And just like Suzanne had warned me during the tour, there was a five-minute limit to my shower.

I made sure to shower quickly.

When I got back to the sleeping quarters, Jessica motioned me to come join her on her bunk. She had a top bunk, and she was sprawled out reading. But she closed her book when I headed her way.

The books were another thing Suzanne had filled me in on during our tour.

There was a bookshelf in the corner of the room, filled with books that had been "approved" by the demons for us to read. Pretty much all of the books were basic romances. None had any science fiction or fantasy aspects, or anything else that might give us any ideas about rebelling. No one knew why they allowed us this small pleasure. It was suspected that they wanted us to spend our extra time reading instead of talking amongst ourselves and possibly discussing ways to escape.

"What are you reading?" I asked as I climbed up to join Jessica on her bed.

She flashed me the cover. It was a man holding a woman up, rain pouring down on them as they were about to kiss. It was a famous book that I recognized instantly.

"I saw the movie," I told her. "Never read the book."

"You can have it once I'm done," she said.

I nodded, even though I didn't intend on spending time reading a mindless romance.

I needed to stay focused on escaping.

"It's good, but it's not why I wanted you to come over here," she said.

I raised an eyebrow, intrigued. "What's up?" I asked, trying to remain as casual as possible.

"I've been thinking about your gift," she said, running her fingers along the edges of the book. "I know we came up pretty clueless during dinner. But when I got back here, I started thinking about what happened here earlier. When Marco had you change into your jumpsuit."

I frowned, not wanting to think about that moment any more than I had to.

But devising an escape meant toughening up and thinking about things I didn't want to think about. So I needed to suck it up and deal with it.

"What about it?" I asked.

"He always delivers the jumpsuits to newcomers," she

said slowly. "He watches them change every single time. He never turns around. Not for me—not for anyone. But for you, he did."

"I asked," I said the first explanation that popped into my mind.

"So did the others."

"Maybe he had somewhere to be and wanted to speed up the process."

"I don't think so," she said. "I haven't been here as long as some of the others, but the first time you change into your jumpsuit is part of the initiation process around here. The demons never turn around. They're demeaning us on purpose. But you told him to turn around, and he did it. It wasn't normal."

"So what do you think my gift is?" I asked. "Persuasive speech?"

It reminded me of what Thomas could do with his vampire prince power of compulsion. He could convince people to do whatever he said.

I'd definitely never been able to do that.

"It would explain why you got Marco to turn around," she said.

"I don't know." I ran my fingers through my hair, not convinced. "If I could do something like that, I think I'd know by now. I mean, I'm usually pretty good at getting what I want. But usually it's because when I want something—when I *really* want something—I stick to my guns and don't back down. People don't just magically listen to me because I want them to. I have to work for it."

"I wasn't saying that's for sure your gift. It's just something to think about," she said as the lights flicked three times above us.

I knew what that meant from my tour with Suzanne. Lights out in five minutes.

"You should probably head over to your bed," Jessica said. "It's rough to navigate in here in the dark. Unless you're Kara, but as far as I'm aware, you don't have a perfect sense of direction. Right?"

"Not even close." I laughed and glanced up at the camera, unease rushing through my body. "So the demons are watching and listening to everything we do." The knowledge was ridiculously unsettling.

"They're watching," she said. "But the cameras don't record audio."

"They told you that?" I asked.

"Thanks to my gift, they wouldn't have told me anything. So I had someone else ask, and I listened in," she said with a mischievous smile. "They told her the cameras recorded audio. It was a lie."

I smiled, since it was the best news I'd heard all day. I

liked Jessica. She was smart and cool. I could see us being friends in the real world.

But I hopped off her bed, not wanting to be stuck navigating in the dark. "Cya at breakfast tomorrow," I said.

"Cya," she replied. "And I hope you like oatmeal. Because we get it every morning."

I made a face—making my feelings about oatmeal clear—and headed over to my bunk.

She was right that I had a lot to think about.

I was also more than ready for lights out. I'd been waiting for it since Suzanne had told me the schedule around here.

Because I planned on using the imprint bond to try contacting Noah.

RAVEN

J lay in my bunk, pulling the threadbare quilt over me and staring up at the ceiling. As expected, the lights went out five minutes after they'd flashed to warn us about bedtime.

It was pitch dark. I tried holding my hand in front of my eyes, and I couldn't see it. The only slim bit of light came from under the door on the other side of the room.

No one said a word, and judging by the light snoring coming from a few bunks away, someone had somehow managed to fall asleep already.

It had been a long time since I'd slept last, and my eyes felt heavy. But I didn't close them. Instead, I focused on the imprint bond—the warm connection between Noah and me that I felt with every beat of my heart.

I wasn't sure how far the imprint bond stretched. I didn't even know where this bunker was. How far was I from Noah right now?

All I knew was that I'd sent him messages through the imprint bond before. Whenever I'd tried, it had worked. Why shouldn't I be able to reach him now?

I tuned into the bond between us, envisioning it as a cord connecting my heart to his. I gathered the energy of the bond and imagined my thoughts flying out toward him.

What was he doing right now?

Trying to find me, I hoped.

There was no knowing if this was working or not. I just prayed it was as I told him everything that had happened to me since being teleported away. I told him about the bunker, about it being Azazel who had taken us, that Sage wasn't with me anymore, and that I needed help escaping.

After recounting everything that had happened since arriving here, I waited.

He didn't reply.

My heart plummeted to the floor. Why wasn't he replying? Had something happened to him?

Was he in an even worse situation than I was in?

If so, we *needed* to get in touch with each other. So I tried again, digging deeper into the imprint bond this time.

I pictured Noah, imagining him being on the receiving end of my thoughts. I focused on the pulsing warmth of the bond until it grew and grew, consuming me completely. I envisioned it reaching out to him, knowing the pulsing was our hearts beating in tandem.

Once I'd enmeshed myself totally into the bond, I went through everything in my mind again, starting from when Sage and I had been taken. The bunker. Azazel teleporting away with Sage. Needing Noah's help.

Again, I waited.

Again, I had no reply.

Defeat hung over my head. But I pushed it away. The imprint bond had worked before. There was no reason for it not to work now.

I refused to stop trying.

And so, I focused on the imprint bond again, and reached out to Noah again. And again. And again.

Each time there was no reply, until eventually I couldn't fight the exhaustion anymore and I drifted off to sleep.

NOAH

Once Thomas ordered the equipment he needed and we pieced our plan into place, we agreed it was best to get some sleep. We needed to be ready to go when the delivery arrived tomorrow.

Amber was about to show us to our rooms when suddenly, the imprint bond around my heart heated up.

I froze in place as thoughts flashed through my mind. Raven's voice.

Trapped in a bunker. Azazel took us. He took Sage. Help.

Her message came to me in impressions, her emotions pulsing through me. Her fear, her desire to get out of wherever she was, her determination, and through it all, her love for me.

My heart panged with how much I loved and missed her.

"Noah?" Thomas stared at me like I'd lost my mind. "Is everything okay? You look like you just saw a ghost."

"It's Raven." I blinked and forced myself to focus on Thomas. "She reached out to me through the imprint bond. She's trapped in a bunker. She says Azazel brought her there, and that he took Sage somewhere else. She needs our help."

Thomas tilted his head, looking torn. Like he wasn't sure whether to believe me or not. "You said we can only communicate through the imprint bond when both people are in the same room as each other," he said. "For anything else, a mate bond is required. Raven contacting you should be impossible."

"That's all true," I said. "But I know what I heard. It was Raven reaching out through the imprint bond. She's worried about me. I need to let her know I'm okay."

The witches said nothing through all of this. They just watched as I sat back down on the couch, glancing at each other curiously.

"Can we get you anything?" Amber asked.

"No," I said. "Just silence, so I can focus."

I closed my eyes and concentrated on the imprint bond between Raven and me. As always, I felt the warmth circling my heart—the warmth connecting me to her.

Feeling it was normal. Using it to connect with her across who knows how far of a distance…

That should be impossible.

But if I wanted it to work, I couldn't let myself think like that. Instead, I focused on sending my thoughts to her.

She'd overcome all known rules of the universe to send a message to me.

Now, I was determined to send one back to her.

I told her how Cassandra couldn't track her, but that Thomas and I were safe in the Devereux mansion. I told her we were trying to get Flint on our side to help us rescue her and Sage from Azazel. But most of all, I told her not to worry about me. I was safe. And until we tracked her down, she needed to stay safe, too. Lastly, I asked if she had any information about the location of the bunker.

Once I knew where she was, I could save her.

As I sent all of this, I felt more connected to Raven than ever. She was there with me. Her feelings and thoughts flowed through my mind like the two of us were one. Well, she was technically always there with me—the imprint bond made sure of that. But now her essence surged over me, like water bubbling over rocks in a stream.

We shouldn't be able to communicate like this. But I

didn't care. Our love was too strong to keep us apart. I knew it, and now the others would all know it, too.

Once I'd told her everything, I waited for a response.

"Well?" Bella crossed her arms over her chest, tapping her foot impatiently.

"I told her everything," I said. "Now we just have to wait—"

I was interrupted when Raven's thoughts flowed over me again.

Joy buzzed through me. But it was quickly followed by defeat.

Because Raven wasn't answering my questions.

She was repeating the same thing she'd said to me before.

I listened to the same story about the bunker. The story about Azazel taking the two of them, and how Raven needed help. None of my questions were answered. It was like everything I'd communicated to her hadn't been received.

"Does she know where Azazel took Sage?" Thomas raised his voice, angry now.

"I don't know." I sat there in a daze, unable to focus on the others around me when Raven felt so close. "She's repeating the same thing from before. The story about how she was taken and where she is. I don't think my message got through to her."

The witches all looked at each other with concern.

"How long has it been since you last slept?" Amber asked softly.

"I don't know." I shrugged and looked to Thomas. I hadn't stopped to think about what time it was since Raven's disappearance.

"It's been over twenty-four hours," he said.

"That's too long," Amber said. "Your system can't function properly on such little sleep. We should all get some rest and regroup in the morning."

"You think I'm making this up?" I glared at her. "You think I'm imagining Raven?"

"I think the stress might be getting to you," she said carefully. "I don't blame you. Ever since Whitney died, there are times when I can feel her with me, too."

"Raven's not dead," I said. "She's alive. And she's communicating with me through the imprint bond right now."

"But you said that's not possible," Bella said.

"It's not." I narrowed my eyes at them, hating them for doubting me. "But it also shouldn't be possible for a shifter to imprint on a human—or on a vampire." I looked at Thomas when I said that last part. "The impossible keeps on happening. Clearly, the rules are changing."

"So reply to her." Thomas stepped forward, his eyes

filled with determination. "Get her to give you more information about this bunker Azazel's keeping her in."

I tried again.

Again, she continued on with the original message, like she didn't hear me at all.

I told the others, and they looked at me with pity. Like I was a child about to have his hopes and dreams snatched from right under his nose.

"Grief and stress can do funny things to our minds, especially when we're sleep deprived," Amber finally broke the silence. "Why don't you go to sleep, and see if you can contact her once you're awake and fresh tomorrow morning?"

"You don't believe me." I sat back in defeat.

How could she think I was imagining this? I'd *heard* Raven. I knew it.

If they could feel what I did, they'd know it, too.

"I never said that," she said, although it was obviously what she was thinking. "But you said yourself that she's not receiving your messages. Maybe you've exhausted yourself to the point where you can't reach her. You'll be better able to help her once you've rested and can get a message through to her."

"Maybe," I said. "I just don't think I can sleep now. Not when our imprint bond feels stronger than ever."

"I bet you'll find that won't be the case once you get into bed," Amber said with a knowing smile.

I looked away from her, overcome by a memory of a similar conversation I'd once had with Raven. It was back at the Montgomery pool house, on the first night we'd met. She'd been through a lot that day, and she needed sleep. But she kept asking me endless questions about the supernatural world. I'd found it annoying at the time. So I told her I'd answer her questions if she could lie down in bed for five minutes and not fall asleep.

She'd fallen asleep in three.

I'd do anything to go back to that moment, when Raven was nearby and safe.

"At least your imprint bond feels strong," Thomas said. "Mine with Sage feels weaker than ever."

"How so?" I asked.

"It feels like it's muffled. I'm worried it means something happened to her..." The vampire prince rarely worried about anything, but in that moment, clear concern radiated in his eyes. "What did your imprint bond with Raven feel like when she was close to death?"

"It didn't change," I said, not sure what he was getting at here.

Did he think Sage was dying?

"But Raven was dying," Thomas said. "I saw her. She

would have died without my help. That didn't affect your imprint bond at all?"

"No." I shrugged, unsure if this was good or bad. "I've never heard of an imprint bond feeling muffled. It's either there, or not. Nothing in between."

"So it doesn't mean she's hurt?"

"I don't know." I wished I could tell him something more helpful. "Maybe it has to do with you being a vampire?"

"Maybe." He didn't look convinced. "But the witches are right—we should get to bed. We have the first part of our plan to put into action tomorrow. We'll be more useful if we're rested and focused."

"Right," I said in a daze, following Amber as she showed us to our rooms.

Once settled in, I lay in bed, listening to Raven sending the same message on repeat. Despite promising the others that I'd get some rest, I continued trying to communicate with her in return.

Each time, I failed.

Eventually, her words stopped, and sometime after that, I drifted off to sleep.

We were awoken the next morning by an annoyingly perky bugle call blasting from the hallway. I groaned and held my hands to my ears, wanting it to stop.

Thanks to Suzanne's "introduction to bunker life" lesson yesterday, I knew what the bugle call meant. We had five minutes to get ourselves up and ready for breakfast. So I grabbed my toiletries basket and hurried to get ready, not wanting to risk standing out by being late.

As warned by Jessica, breakfast was a big bland bowl of oatmeal. It was accompanied by a side of fruit and a glass of orange juice. Like dinner, we were expected to finish every bite.

It was a meal I was familiar with, since the entire

thing was vegan. My mom *loved* making oatmeal in the mornings. I never had a taste for it, but eating it now made me feel closer to her. I'd bet breakfast was her favorite part of the day at this place.

As we dug in, Jessica brought up her theory about my gift being the power of persuasion. The others agreed it was possible, but I still didn't know. It didn't feel right.

Once Harry finished his oatmeal, I tested the theory by telling him to lick his bowl clean. I tried using my "gift" to convince him to do it.

It didn't work.

"Maybe it only works when you *really* want someone to do something," Jessica said. "How badly did you want him to lick his bowl?"

"I wanted him to do it so we could figure out if that was my gift or not," I said. "So yeah, I wanted him to do it pretty badly."

"Hm." Jessica clearly believed me—obviously, because I was telling the truth. She sat back and crossed her arms, looking unsatisfied.

There went that theory.

Once everyone in the cafeteria was finished eating, Marco marched over to our table and hovered over me.

Fear pounded in my chest. I'd been doing everything possible to blend in and not bring attention to myself.

What had I done wrong?

"Number thirty-three," he said, looking down at me. Apparently the demons addressed us by our numbers, and not by our names. "Follow me."

I looked around at the others at my table in alarm.

"It's your assessment with the doctor," Pam said quickly. "Go. You'll be fine."

Of course. Suzanne had told me yesterday that I'd be going to the doctor after breakfast for my assessment.

I took a deep breath and followed Marco out of the cafeteria, trying to get a hold of myself. I needed to be on my a-game. Which meant I couldn't let this place turn me into a frazzled mess.

He led me down the hall. We passed the doors that led to the places Suzanne had shown me yesterday, and he opened one on the end.

The balding man from the cafeteria—the one the others had told me was the doctor—waited inside with a clipboard in hand. The room looked like a regular doctors office, although it was bigger, with some gym equipment inside as well.

"I'm Doctor Foster." His voice trembled as he introduced himself, and he didn't look at Marco or me. "Please take a seat." He motioned toward the examination table, and I did as asked.

Once I was seated, Marco left the room, shutting the door closed behind him.

Now that we were alone, I watched the doctor in anticipation. "I'm Raven," I said, even though he hadn't asked for my name.

He was clearly nervous. Hopefully getting on his good side would help get me information.

He took a seat in the chair across from me, still not looking at me. Instead, he focused on his clipboard and asked a few basic questions, like my age and height. He diligently wrote down my answers, keeping his eyes on his paper the entire time.

It was like he was trying to stop himself from seeing me as a living being.

"Did you take any medications prior to arriving here?" He spoke about this place like it was somewhere I'd chosen to be, instead of somewhere I'd been taken prisoner.

"Just the birth control pill," I said.

"So you're strong in mind?" he asked. "No mental health conditions we need to be aware of?"

"None."

He nodded, apparently content with that response. "Any physical conditions?" he asked. "Prior surgeries?"

"Nope," I said. "Well, I had surgery to get my wisdom teeth out when I was eighteen. Does that count?"

"It doesn't apply to what we need to know here," he said, although he jotted something down just the same.

"What *do* we need to know here?" I leaned forward and held tightly onto the edge of the examination table. "We're prisoners. Why's our health so important? What are the demons getting us ready for?"

Because that had to be what was going on, right? The demons were getting us ready for something?

If they thought they were going to get gifted humans to help in their fight against the supernaturals, they could forget it. I'd never help them. I'd die first.

I'd never felt so strongly about something that I'd die for it, but I hated the demons more than I'd ever hated anyone in my life.

Doctor Foster glanced up at me behind his glasses, pity crossing his eyes. "You and the others here are very, very special," he said slowly. "As I'm sure you already know."

"The others might be special," I said. "I'm not."

"You don't know what your gift is?"

"No idea." I shrugged. "I'd say it was a mistake that I was brought here, but the demons didn't seem to think that was possible."

He wrote my response down, focused on the clipboard again. "We'll figure out what your gift is soon enough," he said. "But let's move onto your family history. Any medical problems—mental or physical—with your parents or siblings that I should know about?"

"You already know my mom." I smiled sweetly, unable to keep the condensation from my tone. "Skylar Danvers. She was here up until a few days ago. You've met her, I assume?"

He looked at me like he was seeing a ghost. "Yes," he mumbled, quickly averting his eyes again. "I did."

"Do you know what happened to her? Where she was moved to?" My emotions were getting the best of me. I was getting over annoyed—and over enthusiastic. But I couldn't help it. I was trapped, angry, and afraid.

Doctor Foster knew what was going on here. He had to. And he was helping the demons.

Why would he do that?

He probably didn't want to do it. He was so skittish that I had a feeling he was being coerced. Which meant he could be on my side. On the side of the gifted humans.

Which meant maybe—just maybe—I could get him to help me.

RAVEN

"Your mother was in excellent health, and was moved to the next location," he said, refocusing on his clipboard. "So there are no health concerns on your mom's side of the family. What about your dad? Siblings?"

"No siblings." I stared at him, trying to will him to open up to me. "And I don't know about my dad. He bolted before I was born."

It was what I always told people. But my dad didn't actually bolt anywhere. He was a guy from another country my mom had hooked up with on vacation. When she told him she was pregnant, he sent her money to get an abortion. But she couldn't bring herself to go through with it. She told him as much, and he said it wasn't his problem since he'd given her the money to take care of it.

As far as I was concerned, he wasn't my problem, either.

People usually felt bad when they found out. But I was fine with it. He might be my biological father, but he was no dad. You couldn't miss something you never had. Well, in this case, some*one*.

Doctor Foster continued on to the physical examination, still not bothering with any small talk.

As he took my weight, height, blood pressure, listened to my heart, had me breathe as long as I could into a machine, and all the other things doctors do, I realized why the best doctors were also good at conversing with patients. This was all extremely awkward with a doctor who refused to acknowledge me as anything other than a specimen to be observed.

The exercise part of the assessment was less awkward, but it kicked my butt.

First he had me run on a treadmill with a heart rate monitor connected to my chest. I'd never been much of a runner. It didn't take long until I was huffing for air and sweating like crazy.

At last he let me stop, only to have me do as many push-ups in a row as possible. I did a few—I think I at least made it to ten—before my arms shook and gave up.

Next was the wall sit. I'd never done a wall sit before, so I had no idea what was good or not. But I didn't reach half a minute before my legs felt like they were on fire.

As for pull-ups, that was impossible. I couldn't do one.

Sit ups, I could handle. Sort of. Same with leg raises. But just when I thought maybe I wasn't completely awful at all this stuff, he had me plank for as long as I could. Which was around twenty seconds, if I was being generous.

The one part I didn't completely flunk at was flexibility. I might not be able to do a push up, but I could touch my toes without bending my knees. Go me.

By the end of it all, my hair was dripping with sweat, and I knew my face was likely as red as a tomato.

"How often did you go to the gym before arriving here?" Doctor Foster asked after finally confirming we were done.

"Never." I used the back of my wrist wipe sweat from my brow. "Obviously."

"Why not?" he asked.

"I was double majoring in psychology and biology." Well, at least that's what I was doing before my memories were erased and replaced and I was forced to take the spring semester off. "Between classes, labs, studying, and sleep, I didn't have time for the gym."

Not like I would have gone anyway, but whatever. I stopped exercising after it was no longer mandatory in high school.

"I remember those days." He glanced off at the far wall, looking slightly happy for the first time since I'd seen him. But whatever bit of happiness he was experiencing disappeared a second later, and he returned to filling out the papers on the clipboard. "Not to worry. I'll get an exercise program ready for you. It'll be delivered to your bed after breakfast tomorrow. You certainly have a long way to go, but I doubt it'll take you nearly as long as some of the others. While you might not have previously enjoyed exercise enough to train to your potential, athleticism is in your blood. Your mom is proof enough of that."

After having my butt handed to me during the assessment, I suspected my dad wasn't athletic at all. He must have given me all of his genes in that area. But I wasn't going to fight the doctor on this one. Especially since he'd just opened up the window to talk about my mom again.

"I know you can't tell me where they took her," I said. "But if I write a note to her, do you think you'd be able to get it to her? Please?" I eyed up the paper and pen in his hand—he had the materials.

I just wanted to communicate with her so she'd

know I was here and okay, and that I'd see her soon. I'd have to be careful about what I wrote—I wasn't naive enough to think the demons wouldn't see the note—but it was better than nothing.

His hands shook around the clipboard, and he looked everywhere in the room *but* at me. "I'm afraid I can't do that," he said. "All I can do is encourage you to strengthen up as quickly as you can. Then you'll be brought to the next location and can see her yourself."

"What do the demons want with us?" I changed angles, since appealing to his emotions clearly wasn't working. "Why do they need us strong to do it?"

Could whatever we were doing in here be the demonic equivalent to the Angel Trials? It would make sense. From the little information I had about the Angel Trials, the point of them was to strengthen us up to become Nephilim.

Was there a demonic equivalent to Nephilim? And if so, were the demons trying to turn us into it?

"I'm not at liberty to discuss this any further." Doctor Foster walked to the door and opened it. "It's time for you to leave, Ms. Danvers. Lunch will be served soon, and I'm sure that after the assessment you just had, you've worked up quite the appetite."

Marco appeared in the hallway, eyeing me up like he didn't like what he was seeing.

Had he been listening the entire time?

I wouldn't be surprised. I also needed to be more careful.

But I'd certainly learned one important thing from that assessment—Doctor Foster wasn't going to give me any information.

Which meant my only hope rested with the other gifted humans.

NOAH

*A*s was customary for supernaturals, the group of us staying at the Devereux mansion was keeping a nocturnal schedule.

But thanks to one day delivery, the equipment Thomas ordered last night was waiting at Amber's doorstop when we woke up the next evening.

Human technology amazed me. For all my life, all I'd known had been the mountains of the Vale. Most of my time there had been spent in my wolf form. Occasionally my pack and I would shift into our human forms, and during that time I heard stories of the outside world. But all they knew of the human world was from before the Great War, which had happened nearly a century ago.

The amount the humans had progressed since then

was remarkable. They'd become more technologically advanced than I could have imagined. I truly would have been lost if Sage hadn't taken me under her wing after I'd arrived in LA.

I hoped that wherever Sage was, she was okay. I didn't want to worry Thomas, but what he said about his imprint bond with her feeling muffled couldn't be good.

I tried again to reach out to Raven through the imprint bond, but I couldn't hear her anymore. At least the imprint bond was still there, which meant she was still alive. But after the way the others had reacted to the message I'd gotten from her last night, they weren't going to believe me unless she sent something I could prove—or if she responded to me.

So I'd just have to keep trying until then.

In the meantime, I went downstairs, ready to help the group with our plan to get Flint on board with our rescue mission.

Empty boxes lined the walls of the living room. Thomas sat in the center of the room, a pile of things he'd called "drones" in front of him. He huddled over one of the drones, doing something or other to it.

I mumbled a greeting to him and walked over to the kitchen, where the delicious smell of bacon was calling my name. Sure enough, Amber and one of her sisters who looked alike—either Evangeline or Doreen—were cooking up a storm in there.

"Evie and I woke up a bit earlier to get breakfast going," Amber said with a smile. "I hope we have enough. We know shifters have crazy large appetites."

I glanced at the sister cooking with her, making a mental note to remember she was Evie and not Doreen.

Evie wore a black shirt with a cat face on it. As long as Doreen wasn't wearing a matching cat shirt when she came downstairs, I'd figure out a more distinct difference between the two witches so I wouldn't confuse them in the future.

"Thanks," I said, practically salivating at the sight of the bacon sizzling on the grill. "Smells great."

Amber tossed me a finished piece of bacon, which I easily caught in my hand and wolfed down.

I wanted to offer to help them out. But cooking wasn't something my pack and I did, since we always ate in our wolf forms. Meaning no cooking required. I hadn't learned at the Montgomery complex because the more submissive wolves cooked there, and on the road Sage and I always ate out or ordered in.

Luckily, my hunting skills made up for my lack of cooking skills.

"It smells fantastic," Thomas said from where he was tinkering with drones in the living room. "But I've gone long enough without blood that it's starting to impair my focus. Which one of your neighbors wouldn't mind me dropping by for a pint or two?"

I glanced at Thomas, noticing that he *did* look paler than usual.

"There won't be a need for that." Bella waltzed down the stairs like a Hollywood diva ready for a day on the set. "Not when you can easily feed on the humans in our basement."

She said it so casually that I did a double take, unsure I heard her right. "Why are there humans in your basement?" I asked slowly.

"Evangeline, Doreen, and I are dark witches," she reminded me. "The most important difference between dark and light magic is one key ingredient. Fresh blood from a human killed by the witch performing the spell or brewing the potion."

"Right," I said, since this wasn't anything I didn't know. "I just didn't realize you kept them in your basement." I looked down at the floor, wondering what types of horrors laid beneath my feet.

I also realized that I didn't know much about the Devereux witches beyond the fact that they'd helped me track demons and also had it out for Azazel after he killed their sister.

Dark witches made up the majority of their circle. Which made them a dark magic circle.

I'd always trusted them because Sage trusted them.

But what if we were wrong in coming here?

"It's inconvenient to have to fetch a human to kill every time we do a spell or brew a potion, so we store them in our basement," Bella said. "But don't worry, dears." She looked back and forth between Thomas and me, apparently noticing the alarm on our faces. "We only capture the worst of the worst. We work with the Tower kingdom in South America and get the most dangerous criminals off the streets. Those monsters down there deserve everything they're getting. You can trust me on that."

"What's in it for the Tower?" Thomas asked.

"Just a small portion of our profit, and a few under the table spells and potions," she said with a smile. "No big deal. So, are you coming or what?"

Thomas must have been pretty hungry, because he stood up and followed her into the apothecary without asking any more questions.

I'd been in there many times, when Amber had done tracking spells to find demons for Sage and I to hunt. I'd always noted the small, padlocked door in the corner—the one the witches never opened. I'd assumed it was where they kept their most valuable materials.

I never would have guessed it led to the basement where they were keeping some of the most wanted criminals in the world so they could kill them at their convenience.

At least they killed criminals and not innocents. Surely that was more than many dark witches could claim. And they were helping us fight the demons. So who was I to judge?

"So," I said, turning to where Amber and Evie were still cooking up a storm in the kitchen. "What can I do to help with breakfast?"

here wasn't much I could do to help out with breakfast. Besides eating it, of course.

Amber and Evie proved to be excellent chefs. Once we'd consumed every ounce of food on the table, I helped the witches clean up while Thomas returned to doing whatever technological stuff he was doing with the drones.

When his work was complete, Bella took the drones into the apothecary and cast a dark magic spell on them to make them soundproof. According to the witches, keeping sound *in* was light magic, and keeping sound *out* was dark magic. So if someone wanted to soundproof a room so someone couldn't spy on them, it was a light magic spell. But if someone wanted something to be soundproofed so they could spy on others, it was dark magic.

In general, that was the basics of how light and dark magic worked. Light magic was more defensive, whereas dark magic was more offensive.

I guessed one of those criminals in the basement had just lived his or her final day.

When everything was ready, we packed up the Devereux SUV with the materials we needed for the task ahead. They had one of those special cars that plugged in and used electricity instead of gasoline.

Thomas was quick to comment about how he owned a few of them as well.

Once we had everything we needed, the witches saw us off. I sat in a passenger seat, and Thomas was behind the wheel. Except he didn't actually need to touch the wheel—or anything in the car—to get it to drive. He just set the radio to a type of music he called "cool jazz," sat back, and used his power to have the car drive on its own.

Show off.

He also didn't need any navigational help, so I was able to sit back and stare out the window. But I wasn't paying attention to the scenery. Instead, I focused on trying to reach Raven through the imprint bond.

By the time we neared the border of the Montgomery property line in the Hollywood Hills, I still hadn't had any luck in contacting Raven. But I could feel her heartbeat through the bond. It was pumping fast— like she was either exercising or panicked about something.

I hoped it was the former, even though the latter was far more likely.

At least she was alive. That was all that mattered. Because as long as she was alive, I could save her and get her back to me where she belonged.

The houses in this area of the Hollywood Hills all had a lot of property to their names, so we stopped at the Montgomery pack's closest neighbor. It was close enough to do what we needed, without getting *so* close that the shifters realized there were other supernaturals near their land. The neighbors were Hollywood stars that Sage claimed were in tons of famous movies, and were always off at some exotic filming location. As expected, they weren't home.

Thomas was easily able to use his power to get us past their gate and situated on their driveway.

We got out of the front seats and walked around to the trunk. Thomas opened the hatch to reveal what he'd dubbed "command central."

The back seats were pushed into the down position to make more room, and it was filled with drones, cameras, controls, and a TV that was wired up and ready to go. There was also a bag full of vials of clear potion—invisibility potion.

Thomas unfolded the first drone and situated one of the cameras inside of it. Then he handed the device to me, and nodded to give me the go ahead.

The unfolded drone looked bizarre—like a giant metallic alien bug posed to attack. It was also much lighter than I'd anticipated from the look of it.

With the drone firmly in my grip, I used my other hand to uncap one of the vials of invisibility potion. I downed it without hesitation. It tasted like nothing, and was light as air.

It tingled as it settled in my stomach, the feeling spreading out to my limbs as the potion did its job of making myself and anything I was wearing or touching with my bare skin invisible. Most importantly, in this case, the drone.

What I could see of my body—and of the drone— was light, hazy, and slightly glowing, like a ghost.

To Thomas and anyone else, I'd be invisible.

He got up, walked to the dirt next to the driveway, and made a circle in the ground with his foot. "Place the drone here," he instructed.

I did as he said, being as careful with the drone as possible. "Done," I said, since Thomas had no way of seeing me. To him, I was a voice coming from nowhere.

With the cloaking ring hiding my scent and the potion hiding me from sight, I was close to the perfect predator right now.

My wolf side wanted to burst onto the Montgomery complex and catch Flint unaware. But I leveled my urges and reined them in. We had the tactical advantage right now, and our plan was good. I couldn't give into my more animalistic instincts when both Raven and Sage's lives were on the line.

Thomas sat back down, remote control in hand, and stared at the television screen in front of him. The screen showed dirt, since that was the view from the camera attached to the drone.

A normal person would have to actually *use* the remote to control the drone. But not Thomas. Simply holding the remote allowed him to "tune into the drone" and lift it off.

As the drone lifted, the view on the television went from dirt to a spanning view of the SUV. The screen showed Thomas sitting in the back, but even though I was there, I didn't show up since I was invisible.

"Looks like everything's working well," I commented.

"Of course it is," Thomas said. "I don't mess up. At

least not when technology's involved."

It was a good thing he'd added on that part about technology, otherwise I would have been tempted to point out that he'd sure as hell messed up when it came to his relationship with Sage.

But there was no need to start a fight with the vampire now, so I pushed the thought aside as the drone zoomed toward the Montgomery compound. I didn't realize I was holding my breath until it was safely over the property line.

When I'd lived there, Flint didn't keep a witch around to maintain a barrier spell around the compound. That hadn't been long ago, but so much had changed recently, especially given the secret alliance he was making. There was no saying how he was protecting the compound now.

Of course, barrier spells were in the shape of a dome. So if there *was* one, Thomas could have flown the drone above it. We just wouldn't have had as good of a viewpoint.

As it was, our view was perfect.

Not just our view—our timing, too.

Because the Montgomery wolves were all gathered in the center of their land in what I instantly recognized as a mating ceremony.

And Sage stood in front, officiating.

NOAH

*R*aven wasn't anywhere to be seen. Which wasn't surprising, since she'd told me through the imprint bond that Sage had been taken somewhere else.

But Sage being here didn't make sense. Azazel had taken her. She knew Azazel had taken Raven as well.

She had to know Thomas and I were worried sick about both of them.

Yet here she was, back home officiating a mating ceremony.

There was no doubt that was what was going on. The Montgomery wolves were all seated in two groupings of chairs, with an aisle in the center between them. Sage stood at the front, with the ritual book in hand.

Why hadn't she reached out to us? What was she

doing here? Why did she look so calm and relaxed, like everything was normal?

And why was she officiating at all? Alphas always officiated mating ceremonies. The only time they didn't was when…

The only time alphas didn't officiate a mating ceremony was when they were the one committing to a mate.

Somehow, I managed to gather my jumbled thoughts together and communicate them to Thomas, who was staring at the screen like he was seeing a ghost. I couldn't blame him. He was *imprinted* to Sage.

If Raven had been safe at home this whole time and hadn't bothered to contact me, I'd be shattered, too.

"The alliance must have something to do with the person Flint chose as a mate," Thomas decided. "He must be holding something pretty huge over Sage's head to get her to go along with this and cease communicating with us."

I nodded, since it made sense. But at the same time, it didn't. "Azazel's the one who took Sage and Raven," I said. "Why would he bring Sage back home?"

"A greater demon took Sage and Raven," Thomas said. "We have no proof it was Azazel."

"Raven told me it was Azazel." I stared straight into

Thomas's eyes, daring him to accuse me of hallucinating that I'd heard her through the imprint bond.

"You're the one who told me imprint bonds don't work like that," he said simply. "Raven couldn't have communicated with you. Therefore, we have no evidence that Azazel is the same greater demon that took Sage and Raven."

Apparently, stare downs didn't work on Thomas like they did on other supernaturals.

One glance down at my hazy hand reminded me that of course it wouldn't work on him. I was invisible.

Thomas had no idea where I was looking.

"Fine." I ran my hands through my hair, since continuing this argument wasn't going to get us anywhere right now. Especially since the ceremony was starting, with Flint walking down the aisle to join Sage in the front. "But we *do* know they were taken by a greater demon. Which still begs the question—why would the greater demon drop Sage back off at home?"

"Maybe she fought him off," Thomas said. "She had that potion on her—the one that forces greater demons to teleport back to their last location. She could have used it on the greater demon and gotten away."

But as he said it, I could tell he didn't believe it. Because if Sage had gotten away, she would have reached out to us as soon as she could.

Just then, Sage glanced up at where the drone was flying.

Her eyes were red. Demonic red. Just like the shifters that had attacked us in the alley.

I didn't need to ask Thomas if he'd seen it. It was clear from the horrified look on his face that he had.

"That bastard is going to pay." Thomas's voice was deadly and terrifying as he stared at the screen. "I don't know what he did to her to make her like that, but he's going to pay."

I wasn't sure which bastard he was referring to—Flint or Azazel—but I nodded in agreement. Because they were both going to pay.

Then I remembered that I was invisible and Thomas couldn't see me nod. Apparently I communicated with my body instead of my words more than I realized.

But I didn't have time to speak before the bride came out of the house. As was customary in mating ceremonies, she was led down the aisle on her father's arm.

Azazel.

When she smiled, her pointed teeth revealed she was a demon as well.

"Shit." I dropped my arms to my sides, dread settling on the bottom of my stomach. "Flint imprinted on a demon."

*I*t all came together in a sudden, horrifying blur.

The alliance Flint had told Thomas about must have been with the demons. That was why he wouldn't tell Sage any details about it. He knew she'd want nothing to do with it. So he'd tried forcing to come back home by getting his allies to abduct her instead.

Quickly, Thomas and I confirmed we'd both come to the same conclusion.

"I can't believe I didn't see it before," he said. "I knew Flint was up to no good. But I never imagined this."

I paced around, unable to stay still. "No one could have imagined this," I said.

"We need to get Sage out of there."

I started to nod, but then I remembered he couldn't

see me. At the same time, I remembered that Sage hadn't made any attempts that we knew of to reach out for help.

She was *smiling* at Flint, Azazel, and Flint's demon bride as she read the opening passages of the mating ceremony.

"Assuming Sage wants to get out of there," I said, the dread in my stomach growing as I watched her.

She was beaming, looking beyond happy to be there.

"She's being forced to marry her brother to a demon," Thomas said. "Of course she wants to get out of there."

I said nothing, not convinced.

"They're holding something over her head to keep her there," he continued. "Otherwise, she'd already be out of there."

"Are you sure?" I didn't want to be the one to say it. But someone had to, and I was the only other one there right now. "We both know Sage. She's not that good of an actress. When she hates someone, it shows all over her face."

Thomas didn't confirm or deny it. He simply stared at Sage on the screen and clenched his fist, looking like he wanted to ram it straight through the glass.

This was the closest the vampire prince had ever come to looking like he was about to lose control.

I wasn't sure what more to say, so I didn't say anything. Anything I could say right now would only infuriate him further. He needed more time to watch—to take in what was right in front of us.

Finally, after a full few minutes of watching Sage happily continue with the ceremony, he broke his silence. "They changed her," he said, his voice a low growl in his throat. "Whatever they did to make her eyes red must have changed her."

He flew the drone around to get another angle of the ceremony so we could see the faces of the Montgomery pack members.

All of their eyes were red.

Only one of them still had normal eyes—a woman I didn't recognize. She wasn't part of the Montgomery pack. But I didn't get much time to look at her before Thomas flew the drone back so it had a perfect view of Sage.

"We need to figure out what the red eyed shifters are," I said. "How they got to be that way, what it does to them, and how to change them back."

Thomas nodded, although the air between us was heavy. This wasn't going to be an easy task.

The Devereux witches knew nothing about the red eyed shifters. And we certainly couldn't burst onto the Montgomery complex and demand answers—not with

Azazel there. The two of us versus the entire Montgomery pack, a demon, and Azazel would be a suicide mission.

We wouldn't do the girls any good if we were dead.

"We'll reach out to as many contacts as we can." Thomas held his cell phone in hand, his expression resolved as he watched the ending of the ceremony on the screen.

Flint and his demon bride made the blood oath to mate with each other that night, and the two of them walked back down the aisle hand in hand.

It was done. Flint had officially promised himself to a demon.

He'd made an alliance with the enemy that wanted all the supernatural races dead.

He might be Sage's brother, but he deserved to burn in Hell for this.

"I just messaged Cassandra telling her everything, so she and the Devereux witches can start researching," Thomas said. "The answers are out there. We just need to find them." He sounded like he was trying to convince himself as much as he was trying to convince me.

"I'm sure they'll find something." My gaze shifted to Azazel as he followed the disgustingly happy couple down the aisle. "But since we're here now, do you know if there's a bunker beneath the Montgomery complex where they might be keeping Raven?"

"I'll see if I can sense one." Thomas pressed his feet to the ground and stared straight ahead, his gaze far off as he focused on using his power. He snapped out of it after a few seconds and looked back to the area where I was standing. "I didn't get anything," he said, and all the hope that Raven might be nearby left my body in an instant. "If there's a bunker, it's guarded with magic and not technology. If it were guarded with technology, I would have felt it."

I nodded, trusting he was telling the truth. I didn't know much about how his power worked, but he had no reason to lie to me.

Then I remembered I was invisible and he couldn't see my motions.

"Thanks for trying," I said gruffly, trying to hide my disappointment.

"Anytime." He shifted his focus back to the screen. "Each drone's battery should last about a half hour each, and we've got a bunch in here ready to go. We can keep this up for another few hours, at the most. We're clearly not going to get any help from Flint like we'd originally hoped, but we should stay here for the rest of the night and spy on them to see if we can get any answers."

"Agreed," I said. "Hopefully we'll hear something

about whatever was done to them to make them this way. Maybe we'll even learn how to help them."

"Hopefully," he said.

And so, we settled into our spots in the trunk of the SUV, ready for the long night ahead.

MARA

J laid in Flint's bed long after our mating was complete, clenching the edges of the comforter in my hands and staring up at the ceiling as I played over the past few hours in my mind.

I wished I could say mating with Flint was everything I'd hoped it would be.

But I couldn't.

After the mating ceremony, we were ushered up to our room, where we could complete the ceremony in private. Making love to seal the bond.

In my dreams, Flint and I would have stayed awake until the sun set, making love until we collapsed into each other's arms in a heap of exhaustion.

In reality, he'd gone through the motions as if performing a duty. He'd barely met my eyes the entire time. I couldn't even call what we'd done making love. Because making love required *emotions.*

Flint didn't appear to have emotions anymore. It was like the person he was had been erased during the blood binding ceremony with my father.

Once we'd gotten up to his room—*our* room now—he'd had sex with me once. Then he'd gotten dressed and said he needed to report to my father to let him know the mating was complete.

I hadn't believed it. I tried seducing him into staying —after all, the Flint I knew and loved couldn't resist me.

But nothing I tried worked. He was like a robot. An empty shell, devoid of emotions. And he was controlled by my father.

What we'd done to him—to *all* of the members of his pack—it wasn't right. We'd destroyed their essences—their souls. I'd played a part in that.

Knowing that I'd played a part in taking away their free will was eating away at me like I couldn't believe. I'd never felt like this before, and I didn't like it.

All I knew was that because of what I'd helped do, Flint was no longer the man I loved.

The man I loved wouldn't have left me alone after our mating ceremony to go serve my father.

I hated to admit I was afraid, but I was. The mate bond had changed something in me.

I *felt* more than I ever had before. It was like every moment up to this one had been muted and dulled. Now my emotions swirled uncontrollably inside of me, making me feel like I was going to shatter from the inside out. I didn't know what to do with all of these feelings. It was like a storm inside me that I couldn't contain, and it positively terrified me.

My kind looked down upon all other creatures. We considered them weak because of their emotions.

Was I now somehow experiencing what *other* creatures felt like?

If so, how did they bear it?

I didn't know. I was starting to feel like I didn't know anything anymore.

So I just lay there, clenching my comforter and staring up at the ceiling, letting the tears roll down my face and not bothering to wipe them away.

RAVEN

*D*inner that night was another "delicious" fare of boiled salmon, plain rice, and unseasoned vegetables. As I sat there, forcing myself to eat every last bite of the bland food, I thought back at everything that had happened to lead up to my being trapped in this place.

I kept going back to when Noah and I had met with Rosella on the Pier. The vampire seer had been very specific about what I needed to do.

She'd said that to save my mom, I needed to go to Avalon, complete the Angel Trials, and become a Nephilim.

Following the doctor's orders and training to go to this "next location" where I'd see my mom again not only misaligned with Rosella's advice, but it sounded too good to be true. And when things sounded too good to be true, they usually were.

I was lucky enough to have been told by a seer how to save my mom. But the path I was currently on didn't match up with the one she had told me I needed to take.

I couldn't let that continue. Maybe I was being silly in putting so much faith into a woman I'd met once, but I didn't think so. Noah had vouched for her, and I trusted Noah's judgment of character. Therefore, I trusted Rosella's advice.

I needed to get to Avalon. This bunker was putting a serious roadblock in that plan.

Which meant I needed to get out of here.

Once I returned to the sleeping quarter after dinner, I told everyone who was in there just as much.

"How, exactly, do you plan on getting out of here?" An older lady whose name I didn't know cackled and held her arms out in amusement. "There's not exactly a door at the end of the hall with a lit up exit sign."

"Yeah," Harry chimed in. "There's nowhere to go."

"Maybe not," I said. "But there are forty of us, and what… four demon guards?" I looked around for verification. I'd only seen four guards so far, but I hadn't been there as long as the others.

"Yep." Jessica walked over and sat next to me on

Suzanne's bed. I took that to mean she was as interested in trying to get out of here as I was.

It made sense. She more than anyone knew the promises of the next location being somewhere we should want to go was a lie.

Now I just needed to get some of the others on board.

"In case you've all forgotten, we're not just humans. We're *gifted* humans." A quick glance around the room showed me I had the attention of others in the bunker, even if they were trying to pretend they weren't listening. "If we put our heads together, we can brainstorm a way out of this."

"You're not the first newbie to think it," Harry said. "It's nothing we haven't tried before."

"What have you tried before?" I asked.

"Nothing that's worked." He shrugged.

"Well, if I know what hasn't worked, it's a better starting point to figure out what *will* work." If he thought he was going to convince me to give up before I'd started, he was thoroughly mistaken.

"You think you're so different than the rest of us," he grumbled. "You're not."

"Do the rest of you have supernatural friends on the outside?" I raised an eyebrow, knowing I'd have them beat there. Sure enough, they shook their heads no. "Shifters, vampires, and witches? Because I do."

All right, I only knew a handful of supernaturals. But it was enough to catch their attention.

After hearing that, some of the others wandered around to where Jessica, Harry and I were talking, including Suzanne and Pam. I counted and saw there were ten people gathered around. Not a huge percentage of people from the bunker, but I could work with it.

Suzanne and Harry remained standing, while the others sat cross-legged on the floor around the bed. I felt like a teacher leading circle time at school.

"Is she telling the truth?" Harry directed the question to Jessica—not to me.

"She is." Jessica smiled—it was the first real smile I'd seen from the girl since I'd met her.

Suzanne watched me cautiously. "How come you're just telling us about this now?" she asked.

"I only learned last night right before lights out that the cameras don't record audio," I said. "Talking about it during the day when the demons are actively patrolling seemed too risky. So I waited until now."

"Makes sense," she said. "Tell us more about these supernatural friends of yours."

Starting from the night my mom was taken, I told about them everything, including the imprint bond between Noah and me. It was hard to talk about Noah without my emotions getting the best of me. But they needed to know about the connection I had with him so they'd understand how important it was for him to get me out of here.

As I spoke, more and more people gathered around, until the group surrounding me had tripled.

"So, are your friends trying to get us out of here now?" Harry asked once I was done.

"I don't know." I bit my lower lip, wishing I could say otherwise. "I tried reaching Noah last night through our imprint bond, but I don't know if he heard me."

"Do you even know if he's still alive?" Valerie asked. She'd been part of the group who had wandered over during my story, although she stood off to the side with her arms crossed.

"If he wasn't alive, the imprint bond between us would be gone," I said. "It's still there. He's alive."

"But he didn't reply back when you tried reaching him."

"No." My heart broke when I spoke the word.

A moment later, an older woman moved toward me and held her hand out for me to take. "Hold my hand," she said. "Then ask if he was able to hear your message."

It was a strange request, and I was sure my expression revealed my confusion.

"It's my gift," she replied. "People can ask me questions. I can feel if the answer is yes, no, or maybe."

"Donna's like a Magic 8-Ball," Jessica chimed in. "But you have to be touching her for her gift to work."

I took a closer look at the woman—Donna—and reached for her hand. Her skin was cold and smooth.

"Did Noah receive my message?" I asked, my heart racing as I waited for her reply.

"Yes," Donna said with a smile. "He did."

"Then why didn't he reply?"

"I don't know." She loosened her grip and pulled her hand out of mine. "My ability only works once per day, and I can only answer yes or no questions."

I frowned, since I'd wanted to ask about my mom as well. But at least I knew Noah *had* heard my message. This was a good thing. I needed to focus on that.

As I was speaking with Donna, a boy and a girl sitting in the circle whispered to each other in what sounded like an argument. They were both thin with matching brown hair and freckles, which made me think they were twins.

The boy said something about how I should "know

about Nancy," and the girl replied saying, "it was totally different."

"Who's Nancy?" I asked, zeroing in on the two of them.

"She was one of the others who was here," the girl—who introduced herself as Kara—said. "She was telepathic."

"She could read minds?"

"Not exactly." She shifted in place, and I motioned for her to go on. "She could get general ideas about what people were thinking and feeling. She could also make people think or feel what she wanted. She was one of the strongest gifted to ever come through the bunker. When she was here, we thought we had a chance of getting out of here."

"What happened to her?" Given that Nancy was no longer here, I had a feeling I wasn't going to like the answer.

"She telepathically connected with the local cops," Kara said. "She asked them to rescue us. Her message got through to them—Donna verified it. But they couldn't help us. The demons killed them all." She wiped a tear off her cheek and looked down at her feet, unable to go on.

"The demons showed us pictures of the bodies to prove it," her brother continued for her. "There wasn't much left of them. They ripped them to shreds. The cops never stood a chance."

"I'm sorry you had to see that," I said, since it had obviously traumatized them. "But those cops were human. My friends are supernaturals. They can fight demons. I've seen them do it before. I've *helped* them do it."

"So you think they're coming to rescue us?" Jessica bounced her legs, looking more excited than ever.

"I'm sure they're trying." I didn't want to get her hopes up too quickly. "I told Noah about the bunker. But Azazel teleported me here, so I have no idea where in the world we are. And Marco said there's a cloaking spell around the bunker, so Noah can't track me. Noah knows I need help, but he doesn't know where to find me. To find *us*." I added on that last part, not wanting them to forget that Noah's searching for me would help them, too.

No one said anything for a few seconds, but a few of them looked to Kara. I did as well.

The girl clearly had something to say. But she pulled her legs up to her chest and wrapped her arms around them, looking scared to say it.

I glanced at Suzanne. Where was her gift of comfort when we needed it?

Apparently understanding what I wanted, Suzanne

walked over to Kara and placed a hand gently on her arm.

"Nancy was able to tell the cops where we were because of me," Kara finally said softly. "Because of my gift. They're dead because of me."

"No," I said, hating that she felt that way. "You and Nancy were doing a good thing trying to help everyone trapped in here. You're not responsible for the deaths of those cops. The demons are." I paused, wanting to be patient with her. But if she knew where we were, I needed to know so I could send the location to Noah. The sooner, the better. "But like I said earlier, Noah has a special weapon that can kill the demons. He's killed nine demons with it so far. If there's anyone out there who can save us, it's him."

"He didn't kill those nine demons all at once." Kara raised her eyes to meet mine. While she was young, her gaze shined with intelligence. "He's only killed one at a time."

"True. Which is why I'll tell him there are four demons here, so he'll come prepared with backup," I said. "I just need you to tell me where this bunker is. Can you do that?"

She glanced at her brother.

He shrugged, as if saying *why not*, and Kara looked back over to me. She lowered her arms from around her knees and straightened her shoulders, looking stronger and more confident. She looked like she'd made a decision.

I hoped it was in my favor.

"I can give you the exact coordinates," she said with a knowing smile. "Because my gift is a perfect sense of direction."

NOAH

*T*homas and I stayed out all night, using the drones to spy on the Montgomery pack. Each time a drone ran out of battery, he'd call it back. Then I'd take invisibility potion while holding a new drone and we'd send it out to continue filming.

By the time the sun was about to rise, we hadn't learned anything we didn't already know from watching the mating ceremony between Flint and Azazel's daughter. All I'd gotten was an irritating stomachache from drinking so much invisibility potion.

It wasn't advised to drink more than one potion in twenty-four hours. Doing so wouldn't harm me long term—the witches had promised me that—but I'd feel nauseated until it was out of my system. Which was a new experience for me, since supernaturals don't get sick. At least not with the same illnesses as humans.

Thomas packed up the last drone, and I took the antidote tablet to make me visible again. Unfortunately, the antidote tablet didn't cure my stomach. The only cure for that was time.

When we got back to the Devereux mansion, they had boxes of delivery pizza waiting for us.

Seeing the boxes of pizza reminded me of Sage. Delivery was our go-to meal when we were on the road demon hunting. That girl could eat more slices than I could.

Damn, I was worried about her.

"Hopefully you like pizza," Amber said. "I got one with all meat toppings on it, just for you." She looked at me when she said that last part, and I nodded in thanks.

"We've been researching the red eyed shifters all night," Cassandra said. "The library here has so much information—some I'd never seen before. They told me I could copy some for the library at the Bettencourt once this is all over."

"What did you find out?" Thomas asked.

"Let's sit down." Bella made her way over to the table. "We'll talk over dinner."

Despite it being a casual meal of delivery pizza, that hadn't stopped the girls from bringing out the fancy plates and glasses. And judging by the martinis in four spots, the red wine in two others, and the beer in the other, they'd decided on our seating arrangements, too.

We all took our seats, and I opened the box Amber told me was mine. It looked and smelled delicious— loaded with every type of meat available.

Hopefully it would soak up the potion swirling around in my stomach.

Amber took a slice of plain pizza, placed it on her plate, and cut into it with a fork and knife. I couldn't help looking at her like she was crazy.

"What?" she asked.

"I've just never seen anyone eat pizza with a fork and knife before," I said.

"Enough," Thomas said, and all eyes went to him. He was seated, but he hadn't moved to touch the food. "We need to know everything you learned about the red eyed shifters. Sage's life depends on it."

The witches looked at each other and said nothing. It was like they were silently debating who was going to speak first.

If they knew something that could help, they'd be jumping to share.

I took a swig of my beer and braced myself for the worst.

Bella was the first to eventually speak. "Like we

suspected, the red eyed shifters are a result of ancient, dark magic," she said. "There haven't been any on Earth for a few millennia, but we found a mention of them in an old book from the back of our library. Back then, they were called slaves to the demons. They were all killed once the demons were banished to Hell. No one has mentioned them since."

"Do you know how they became that way?" I asked. "Or how to change them back?"

"No." She shook her head sadly. "The only witches who could answer that question are the ones in the family that created the spell all those thousands of years ago. Their knowledge of the spell must have survived. And apparently they're working with the demons— either by choice or force—which is how demon slaves are being created now."

I barely heard what she was saying, because my imprint bond with Raven suddenly ignited. She was sending me another message.

Numbers, in a loop. So many numbers.

I slammed by hands down onto the table, and all eyes went to me.

"Write down the numbers I tell you to," I commanded, not speaking to anyone in particular. "Now."

NOAH

*A*mber took charge, writing the numbers on a napkin.

"These are the coordinates for the bunker where Raven's being kept," I said once they were written down.

The others looked at me with a mix of shock and awe.

"I told you she was communicating with me through the imprint bond." I couldn't help sounding smug. They deserved it, after how easily they'd dismissed the possibility yesterday.

Thomas brought his phone out and stared at it. "These coordinates place Raven about thirty miles outside of Aurora, Nebraska," he said. "There's a farm there with a small house on the property. The coordinates are near the house, but not exactly inside of it."

"She wouldn't be *in* the house," I said. "The bunker would be *underneath* the house."

"Why would there be a bunker underneath a farm in the middle of nowhere?" Amber scrunched her nose, as if the thought of living in such a place disgusted her.

"A tornado shelter?" Evie guessed.

"A hidden witch circle practicing ancient dark magic?" Doreen said.

"A human family preparing for the apocalypse?" Bella voiced her theory. "Some humans do that, you know. I watched a documentary on it once."

The witches widened their eyes and smiled, clearly enjoying this little brainstorming session.

I slammed my hands on the table, bringing everyone's attention back to me. "It doesn't matter why the bunker exists. All that matters is that Raven's there." I turned my focus to Thomas, not wanting to lose a second of time that could be spent helping Raven. "Bunkers have security systems, right?" I asked, and he nodded in confirmation. "Any chance you can tap into this one?"

"I can," he said. "But not with the limited equipment we have here."

"Where, then?" I asked.

"We'll have to go back to the Bettencourt."

Cassandra teleported Thomas back to his penthouse at the Bettencourt, and Bella teleported me there.

At least, Bella *tried* to teleport me there. Apparently, witches weren't accurate with teleporting to places they'd never been before.

We ended up landing in the center of the hotel restaurant. It was just past sunrise on a weekday, so it wasn't busy. But a few people wearing business attire who were indulging in a large breakfast buffet looked at us strangely.

"Come on." Bella didn't let go of my hand as she led me out of the restaurant and toward the elevator. She walked confidently, as if she belonged there.

I glanced behind us at the people who had already stopped paying us any attention. "Aren't they going to wonder how we appeared out of thin air?" I asked once we stepped into the elevator. Luckily we were the only two people in it, so I was able to speak candidly.

"Most humans are remarkably good at rationalizing away magic, even when it happens right in front of their eyes. They'll assume we were there the entire time, or that they just didn't notice us until then." She perused the panel of buttons, not pushing any of them. "Thomas said he lived in the penthouse. Should I assume the top floor is his?"

The elevator zoomed up before I could answer. "Apparently he already spotted us," I said.

The doors opened straight into the foyer of Thomas's penthouse.

It felt like forever since I'd last been here, even though it had only been two days.

"Your appearance in the middle of the restaurant showed up on the security cameras," Thomas said, not looking bothered in the slightest. "But don't worry. My coven is already taking care of it with memory potion."

"That was hardly necessary, given that we barely caused a stir." Bella marched into the living room and sat down on the couch, making herself at home. In her sleek, all-black outfit and matching high-heeled boots, she looked like she belonged there. "Humans use 'logic' to explain away magic all the time."

"As the largest rogue vampire coven in North America, we take every precaution to remain undetected," he said. "Now, if you'll excuse me. Tapping into the security system of a place miles away from here is do-able, but not easy. I'm going to need time in my study to figure this out."

"How much time?" I asked.

"A few hours, at the most."

"Hours?" I couldn't believe it. Now that we finally had a solid lead on Raven, I wanted it to take *minutes* not, hours. Hours seemed like an impossibly long time to sit around waiting.

"Unless you don't want my help at all?" He raised an eyebrow. "My debt to Raven has already been paid. I'm helping you now because you just spent the night spying on the Montgomery complex with me for Sage. But if you don't want my help…"

"Of course I want your help," I said, stopping him from being ridiculous. "Is there anything we can do to help speed up the process?"

He gave me a hard stare that I assumed meant no. "Just wait here," he said. "And try not to break anything."

*A*s Thomas worked in his study, Bella, Cassandra, and I had a frustratingly circular discussion about why Azazel would want Raven in a bunker, and about why Sage would so easily support her brother's alliance with Azazel and become a slave to the demons.

We were pretty clueless about why Raven was being kept in a bunker. As for Sage, Bella was convinced she'd been playing us all along, and that she'd been siding with the demons the entire time.

Cassandra and I adamantly fought against this theory. Sage might be a rule breaker (okay, she was *definitely* a rule breaker), but her heart was in the right place. She'd never side with the demons. At least not willingly.

"Her brother imprinted on a demon—on Azazel's daughter," Bella pointed out for the third time since we'd gotten here. "I've worked with enough shifters to know they value their pack above all else. And Flint isn't just a member of the pack. He's their alpha." She paused, like she was trying to be as dramatic as possible. "When the alpha makes a major decision, their pack either follows or gets cast out. I know you were both close to Sage. But is it so crazy to think she would fall in line and stick with her pack, even if it went against her better judgment?"

I was about to call Bella out on the fact that she was acting like she knew more about my own species than I did.

But Thomas chose that exact moment to emerge from his study.

Bella didn't see him because her back was toward him. She was also halfway through her second martini since we'd gotten here, which I assumed was dulling her supernatural senses a bit.

"It *is* crazy to think Sage would do such a thing," Thomas said, and Bella rolled her eyes before turning around to face him. "Especially considering that Flint isn't her only family. She imprinted on me. If her pack cast her out, she'd always have a home at the Bettencourt. She knows that."

"Fine, fine." Bella rested an elbow into the back of the couch and took another sip of her drink. "It was just a thought. I won't bring it up again."

I eyed up Thomas, hope lighting up my chest at what his emergence could mean. It had only been an hour and a half. But maybe for once the universe was on our side here.

"Did you get into the security system?" I stood in anticipation of his answer.

"The system was more rudimentary than expected," he said. "So yes. We're in."

He led us into the media room and brought up a video on the big screen television. The video was black and white and slightly grainy, but there was Raven, sitting on the bottom bunk of a bed. About twenty people surrounded her, listening to whatever she was saying. Some of them sat cross-legged on the floor, and others stood. All of them wore what looked like prisoner jumpsuits.

But I barely paid attention to the others. My entire focus was on Raven. Relief coursed through my body at how healthy she looked. Up until now, I'd feared she'd been experiencing terrible treatment from the demons. Beating, torturing... it hurt too much to think about, so I'd pushed the possibilities from my mind.

Seeing that she appeared in good physical shape put aside those worries for now.

The group was talking about something, but I only knew that because their lips were moving. I couldn't hear a thing.

"Is there any sound?" I asked.

"Like I said, the system is rudimentary," Thomas said. "The cameras are decades old. They don't record audio —only video. It's like whoever owns this bunker hasn't updated it since it was built."

Suddenly, the lights on the screen flickered. It must have meant something to them, as the people around Raven headed toward what I assumed were their own beds.

Raven spoke for a bit with a teen girl sitting next to her—it killed me that I couldn't hear what they were saying—until the girl eventually got up and went to her bed as well. Then Raven stared up at the camera, and my heart stopped.

I could feel through the imprint bond that she was thinking of me. That she was hoping I was searching for her.

I tried again to reach out to her through the bond and let her know I was. Maybe it would work now that I could actually see her.

She gave no signs of receiving my message. She just climbed onto the top bunk and curled up to go to sleep.

Less than thirty seconds later, the camera went dark.

"What happened?" I looked to Thomas, panicked. "Where'd the video go?"

"Relax," he said. "The lights went out in the bunker. The camera is still working. See that light on the edge?"

I looked to where he was pointing and nodded.

"That's the light from the hall peeking out from under the door," he said. "Like I said, this camera system is rudimentary. It doesn't have night vision."

I stared at the screen, endless questions running through my mind. I wanted to know so much. But for now, I needed to focus on helping Raven.

"Is that the only room in the bunker?" I asked.

"No," Thomas said. "There are a few more. A cafeteria, a kitchen, a gym, a communal bathroom, and what looks to be a doctor's office. And the hall, of course." He used his power to flip through the camera views as he spoke about them. "There appear to be four demons guarding the facility."

Four demons versus Thomas, Cassandra, and me. There would be even more on our side if the other Devereux witches agreed to help. Judging from their desire to defeat the demons, they would.

We had the numbers to defeat the demons and break out the humans.

This was assuming the demons guarding the bunker weren't greater demons, but I doubted they were. There weren't many greater demons in existence. And from what I'd seen, greater demons didn't venture out to scout for humans to kidnap or guard bunkers. That was what their demon minions were for.

Since Azazel had brought Raven to this bunker, I'd bet these guard demons worked for him.

"Now we have to study everything about this place and make a plan to break in." I rubbed my hands together, ready to get started. "Because we're getting Raven—and all the other kidnapped humans—out of there."

NOAH

"A few minutes of seeing Raven, and you've already forgotten about Sage," Thomas said coldly. "I should have known this would happen."

"I haven't forgotten about Sage," I said.

"Could have fooled me," he replied. "Perhaps I shouldn't have hacked into the bunker security system until we got Sage back home. That would have given you enough incentive to remember she needs our help too. Don't you think?"

I jumped up with my arms out, ready to throttle him.

Someone leaped in front of me and wrapped their hands around my wrists, holding me in place. Bella.

Witches were generally the most peaceful of the supernaturals. It made it easy to forget that they could hold their own against us. And while I wasn't actually trying to harm Bella, I was impressed by her strength.

Cassandra had raced to Thomas's side, although the vampire prince hadn't done as much as flinch. The man was like a damned robot. The fact that Sage had fallen in love with and imprinted on him baffled me.

The two of them couldn't be more opposite if they tried.

"We're all on the same side here," Bella said, her grip firm around my wrists. "I doubt either Sage or Raven would want the two of you trying to rip each other to shreds when they *both* need your help."

"He wouldn't have been able to harm me." Thomas smiled, his teeth glinting even in the low lighting. "But it would have been interesting to see him try."

A growl rumbled deep in my throat. I *wanted* to try.

But Bella was right. No matter how badly I wanted to wrangle Thomas, I had to focus on helping the girls. We all did.

And I *did* have logical reasons for wanting to save Raven first. Yes, I also had personal reasons. But saving her first made sense.

To get Thomas to understand, I'd have to do it in his language. Facts and logic.

I could do it. I *had* to do it. For Raven.

Bella must have felt my tension ease, because she loosened her hold on my wrists. "You good now?" she asked.

"Yeah." I nodded. "I'm good."

She let go and stepped to the side, although she looked ready to jump back in front of me in case I launched myself at Thomas again.

I rubbed my wrists where she'd been holding them. She had a strong grip, which was good. She'd be more of a help in battle than I'd initially realized.

Thomas examined me coolly. "Don't try that again," he warned.

"Don't use Raven as a tool to threaten me." I held my gaze with his to show I wouldn't back down. There were certain limits I wouldn't tolerate being crossed.

Thomas dangling Raven's safety in front of me like a carrot to get me to do his bidding was one of those limits.

"I was simply saying what was necessary to ensure you didn't forget about your so-called best friend, Sage," he said—as if I needed reminding about her existence.

"I didn't forget about Sage." I sat back down on the couch, although I didn't get too comfortable. "We'll get Sage out of there. But Raven *asked* for our help. She reached out to me through our imprint bond—a feat that should be impossible—and asked us to rescue her. She's being unwillingly kept in a bunker where she's likely in mortal danger from the demons."

Thomas regarded me with pure disdain. "Are you presuming Sage isn't in mortal danger from the demons as well?" he asked.

"Sage appeared to be willingly cooperating with Azazel," I said. "We don't have much to go on regarding her red eyes, but it seems like she's bound to the demons. Why would they harm her further after going through the trouble of binding her to them?"

"It's a fair point," Bella said. "In the book my sisters and I found, there was no mention of the demons harming the shifters who were bound to them. In fact, they protected them. Like family pets."

Anger flooded my veins at the thought of anyone treating Sage like a "family pet."

"Even more of a reason to get Sage out of there," Thomas said. "She hates being coddled and told what to do."

"She's also not in mortal danger," I reminded him. "We need more information about the demon bound, specifically how to break the bond. And we'll find it. But for now, Raven has asked for immediate rescue. We have the information and manpower to accomplish that.

Then, once Raven's secure, we can put all our resources into freeing Sage and her pack from this bond with the demons. I don't know how long that's going to take. But it's going to take time. Which is why it makes sense to focus on saving Raven first."

Thomas pressed his lips together, saying nothing.

Had my appeal to him worked?

The vampire prince turned to Cassandra, who had been quiet throughout all of this. "What do you think?" he asked her. "Will it take as long to figure out what's going on with the demon bound shifters as the Devereux witches and Noah think?"

Cassandra looked at me, then at Bella, and finally back to Thomas. "It certainly won't be simple," she said. "We barely have any record of demon bound shifters, and we don't know which dark magic family created the spell. Even if we do figure out the family, I doubt they'll hand over the details about reversing it willingly."

If it can be reversed, I thought, although I didn't say it out loud. I suspected we were all thinking it.

There was no need for negativity at a time like this.

"So you agree with Noah," Thomas said flatly.

"Sage's rescue is going to come with its fair share of complications," she said. "I don't think Raven's will be simple, but it certainly seems more straightforward."

"I agree with Noah and Cassandra," Bella voiced her

opinion, even though Thomas hadn't asked for it. "We'll rescue Raven first. We're one kick ass group of super-naturals—we've got this. Once Raven's safe we can put our heads together and figure out how to move forward with Sage and the rest of the Montgomery pack."

I hadn't known her long, but I was getting the impression that Bella was the type of woman who wasn't afraid to speak her mind.

She and Raven would get along well. I couldn't wait for them to meet.

I looked back over at Thomas, unsure what to say to add to my point. The facts were all out there.

But I was asking a lot from him, and he didn't owe me anything.

"Your gift with technology will be instrumental in saving Raven," I said, since I needed to say *something*. "Getting into that bunker will be much harder for us without you. Then, once Raven's safe, I'll do everything in my power to help Sage. She risked her life to help me on my demon hunt, and I love her like family. I won't abandon her. You have my word."

Thomas watched me carefully as I spoke, his eyes hard.

I feared he was about to say no. I sat straighter and clenched my fists, preparing for the worst.

"If you'd asked me a week ago, I'd have said that the

word of the First Prophet meant nothing," he finally said. "But after the past few days, I believe you're an honorable man who will follow through on your promise."

"So you're in?" I held my breath, not wanting to get my hopes up before he agreed out loud.

"Now that I've tapped into the bunker's security system, I can easily connect it to the devices in the Devereux home. We can all watch what's happening in the bunker from there," he said. "I've set the cameras to record everything. Once we discern a pattern in how the demons are running the place, we can create a plan to break in. I've faced far worse challenges in the past. I hardly imagine this one will prove difficult."

That was a yes. He was going to help us.

Elation warmed the imprint bond around my heart, making me feel like Raven was right there with me.

But I did my best to appear as cool and collected as Thomas. He was doing a lot by helping us. There was no need to rub my happiness into his face.

"That sounds like a solid plan," I said. "Then, once Raven's safe, we'll focus on Sage. We *will* break that bond she has with Azazel. I wouldn't be able to live with myself if we didn't."

"That makes two of us." Thomas stood, wiped invisible lint from the sleeve of his suit, and held out his hand to shake mine. "So we have ourselves a deal?"

I stood as well, reaching for his hand and giving it a firm shake. "Yes," I said, holding my gaze steady with his. "We do."

THOMAS

I'd told the others that I agreed to wait to rescue Sage until breaking Raven out of the bunker.

I'd lied.

Now, we were all back in the Devereux mansion. Everyone had retired to their rooms to sleep for the day, so we'd be ready to devise a plan to rescue Raven the next night.

Not me.

Well, I'd gone to my room. But I hadn't gone to sleep.

Instead, I sat at the desk inside the room, writing Sage a letter.

I'd already tried calling her, texting her, and sending an email. It had all gone unanswered or unread.

I assumed she was being cut off from all technological methods of communications. It was likely her brother's doing. Or Azazel's.

I shuddered at the thought of the greater demon, and how Sage had beamed at both him and his demonic daughter as she'd officiated his daughter's mating ceremony to Flint.

There was no way Sage wanted to be there. Yes, she was bound to the demons, but I knew Sage. She was too strong to give in that easily.

Which was why I was writing her this letter.

No one should have to go through what she was going through alone. Our imprint bond might be dulled, but it was still there. If I couldn't communicate with her through the imprint bond, and I couldn't communicate with her through technology, then I'd resort to old school methods.

Good old pen and paper.

In the letter, I told her how much I loved her, and that I'd do anything to help her escape the Montgomery compound and break the demon bond. I let her know I was in LA, and asked her to sneak out to meet me at a specific place and time the next day.

Sage would figure out a way to sneak out. She'd sneaked out of the Bettencourt enough times as a teen that I trusted her ability to be stealthy. Of course, I'd known she was sneaking out back then because of all the cameras in the hotel, and I'd had her followed to ensure she was safe.

She'd rise up to the challenge. I knew she would.

Once I signed the letter, I gathered the supplies I'd need for my outing into a large backpack. One of the drones that had been given the soundless spell, plus a vial of invisibility potion and its antidote that I'd taken from my stash before leaving the Bettencourt.

No one had blinked an eye when I'd taken the drone up to my room when we'd returned, under the claim that I might want to tinker with it more to make improvements. They hadn't noticed that I'd taken the backpack it had arrived in, either.

Since I had no choice but to do this in the daytime, I dressed to cover as much of my skin as possible. It was a myth that vampires combusted into flames in the sun. We couldn't be killed that easily. But the sun *did* sap our energy. It also gave us sunburn, and while we healed from it quickly, it was still painful. That was why we kept a nocturnal schedule.

Going out in the sun would be draining no matter what. But keeping my skin from getting hit with direct rays would reduce its effects.

Next was the trickiest part of the plan—because it was the only part that relied on anything other than technology and myself.

As quietly as possible, I left my room and walked down the hall. Once I reached Cassandra's room, I opened the door and let myself inside.

As suspected, the lights were off and Cassandra was fast asleep. Her long brown hair was a mess on her pillow, and she didn't wake when I entered. She'd always been a heavy sleeper.

I clicked the door quietly in place and walked over to her bed, placing a hand lightly on her shoulder to wake her. She remained sleeping. So I nudged her a bit harder —hopefully not so hard as to frighten her.

Her eyes popped open and met mine in question.

She opened her lips to speak, but before she had a chance, I held my phone out in front of her. On it, I'd already written a message.

Put up a sound barrier spell so we can speak freely.

She nodded, sat up, and muttered a repetition of words under her breath in Latin.

"Let me guess," she said once the spell was complete. "You're not waiting to help Sage until after Raven is rescued?"

"You know me too well." I smiled wickedly. While all of my immediate family was dead and could obviously never be replaced, Cassandra had always felt like a sister to me. I wasn't surprised she knew what I was up to before I had a chance to tell her.

"What's the plan?" she asked, the question quickly followed up by a yawn.

It was a good thing the plan didn't depend on her being able to stay awake, because then she'd definitely fail.

I told her everything I was going to do, and she listened, not looking surprised in the slightest.

"Here's where you come into play," I said once I'd given her the gist of it all. "I can easily get past the technology of this house to sneak back inside. But I can't get past the magical barrier."

"So you'll need someone on the inside to get you through," she finished.

"You got it," I said. "Think you can handle it?"

"As long as you call me to wake me up when you're heading back," she said. "Because I'm way too tired to stay awake waiting."

"Consider it done." I'd expected as much, since Cassandra made it no secret that she couldn't function without at *least* eight hours of sleep a night.

"Oh, and Thomas?" she asked as I made my way out. I looked back at her, and she continued, "I'm glad you're doing this for Sage. I know she'll be grateful, too." Then she paused and pressed her lips together, making me nervous.

"What?" I asked.

"I just hope you're prepared that Sage might be different."

"Different how?" I asked.

"I was there with the Devereux witches reading up on the demon bound in their library," she said. "While there's not much written about them, it sounded like they were all loyal to their demonic masters."

"Sage hates Azazel." I inwardly reeled at the thought of anything else. "She'd never be loyal to him."

"I know." She hunched over slightly, looking like she regretted saying anything at all. "Just be careful. All right?"

"You know me," I said. "I'm always careful."

With that, I left her room and headed out of the mansion, eager to get to the Hollywood Hills and get my letter to Sage.

MARA

Someone knocked on the door, jolting me out of a deep sleep.

Flint sat up in the bed beside me. He was instantly alert.

I stretched and rubbed sleep from my eyes. It was before sunset. Who was awake at this hour? And why were they knocking on our bedroom door?

Sit up, Flint's voice echoed in my mind. Now that we were mated, we could communicate telepathically without the strain it had taken when we only had the imprint bond between us. *We need to put up a united front.*

Despite the heaviness in my head from being woken so suddenly, I also sat up in bed.

Who is it? I sent the thought into Flint's mind instead of speaking aloud. My sense of smell wasn't as heightened as a shifter's. I could discern between different supernatural species, but Flint could smell the subtle differences between each member of his pack.

Likely Sage, he replied. *Whoever is on the other side of that door is cloaking his or her scent. Sage is the only one of our pack permitted to wear a cloaking ring right now.*

Right, I thought—to myself and not to Flint. At least the mate bond didn't let him into my head *all* the time. He only heard what I wanted him to hear.

My father had commanded the Montgomery pack members to remove any cloaking talismans, so he'd know where they were at all times. They were quick to comply. The only pack member permitted to remain cloaked was Sage. My father didn't want anyone knowing where she was right now.

It didn't make sense. If he wanted those who were looking for her dead, wouldn't he *want* them to track her? Then they'd come right to him.

I'd asked him such. But he'd simply reassured me there was a long-term plan in place and told me to stop asking questions.

"Come in," Flint called out, his strong voice bringing me out of my thoughts and back into the present.

As he'd predicted, Sage walked through the doors. Her red eyes were devoid of emotion, just like Flint's had been ever since the blood binding ceremony. And she carried a strange creature in her hands. A giant, multi-legged bug made of metal.

I sucked in a deep breath and widened my eyes, not liking the look of the thing. "What is that?" I kept my eyes locked on it, poising myself to jump up and run in case it attacked.

"Don't look so frightened," Sage said, her voice flat. "It's a drone. Human-made technology. It's not going to hurt you."

I relaxed, but only slightly. Human-made or not, I still didn't like the look of it. "What's it doing here?" I asked.

Flint spoke before Sage had a chance. "Thomas Bettencourt has something to do with this," he said. "Doesn't he?"

I knew who Thomas was. Flint had told me about him back when he was still himself, before going through with the blood binding ceremony.

Thomas and Sage had been planning on getting married, but Flint didn't think the pairing was practical. He wanted Sage to find her true mate.

So he'd gone to Thomas and voiced his concerns. It turned out Thomas had similar concerns. Flint told Thomas he didn't support the marriage, and vowed to kick Sage out of the pack if the two of them went through with it.

Thomas didn't want to make Sage choose between him and her pack. So he'd broken the engagement and made the decision for her.

When Flint had first told me the story, it sounded perfectly logical.

Now, my heart went out to Sage. From what I knew, she and Thomas had truly been in love. What harm was their love causing anyone? Why should she have been forced to choose between her pack and the man she was in love with?

The thought both surprised and scared me.

Before, I hadn't cared at all.

Why did I care now?

It was yet another alien emotion that made me wonder if the mate bond between myself and Flint had changed something in me—something that went down to the root of my soul.

"It was Thomas." Sage spoke his name with no emotion—like her love for him had been erased. "He must have flown it through my window last night while I was sleeping. It has a sound proofing spell on it, so I didn't hear it arrive."

"How did he know you were here?" Flint's eyes narrowed, and he continued before Sage could answer. "If you told him we're here, admit to it now. I can't promise how Azazel will react, but I'll ask for him to go easy on you since you came clean on your own."

"I didn't tell Thomas I was here." Sage looked surprised Flint would even think it. "Azazel wants my location to remain secret. I would never betray his trust. Not after everything he's done for us."

Flint nodded, apparently believing her.

I believed her, too. She sounded so cold and heartless it was impossible not to.

"Then how did he know you're here?" Flint asked.

"I don't know," she said. "But there was a letter attached to the drone." She placed the thing—the *drone*—down on the floor and removed the letter from her back pocket. "I apologize for waking both of you so early, but I thought it best to deliver the letter to you straight after finding it."

"The letter was addressed to me?" Flint looked perplexed.

"No," she said. "It was addressed to me. But Thomas doesn't realize I'm here willingly. He asked me to betray Azazel and our pack. I thought it best to immediately deliver the letter to you—my alpha—so you can decide what to do about it."

"You thought correct." Flint raised his hand and motioned for her to come forward. "Give me the letter so I can read it myself."

She did as asked.

Flint opened the letter and read it. He allowed me to read it over his shoulder. The handwriting was exquisite, but slanted, as if written in a rush.

Dearest Sage,

I've never been the best as expressing my emotions. That was always where you shined. But seeing you snatched away from me broke me in ways you can't begin to imagine.

I was supposed to keep you safe, and I failed. I'll never be able to forgive myself for that. Especially knowing that because of my ineptitude, you were forced to become a slave to Azazel.

I have sources working on figuring out how to break this bond between you two. I just hope you know that no matter what he's done to you, it doesn't change the way I feel about you. I love you Sage. I always have, and I always will. The imprint bond between us has grown weak, but it's still there. Our love cannot be broken.

I was foolish enough to let you get away from me twice. It won't happen a third time. I promise you that.

I have eyes on the Montgomery compound. I saw how well you're pretending to go along with what that monster is doing for you. It's a smart decision, and I'm proud of you for making it. It's kept you alive. But you won't have to pretend for much longer. Because I'm here for you, and I'm going to keep you safe from now on.

I'd march inside the compound right now and take you away to safety if I thought we could get out of there alive. But it would only get us both killed.

So you're going to have to sneak out of there yourself. Since you have them all convinced you're on their side, I know you can do this. I love you, and I believe in you. All of your rebellious experience of sneaking out of places in the past will finally come in handy, just like I always knew it would.

But you have to do it soon. Tomorrow, during the day, when everyone is asleep.

Meet me at the place you wanted to take me when I visited you in LA. I'll be waiting for you at noon.

I love you, always,

Thomas

PS: Once you read this letter, burn it. We can't risk anyone finding it.

PPS: I love you.

MARA

I'd never met Thomas, but I could practically feel his love for Sage oozing off the pages.

He loved her as much as Flint had loved me before the blood binding ceremony with Azazel.

Flint looked up from the paper, his red eyes raging with anger. "You imprinted on Thomas?" he asked, barely containing his fury.

"I don't know." Sage shrugged, looking truly clueless. "He claims so in the letter. But I don't feel the bond between us. The only bond I feel is the one with Azazel."

Dread twisted in my stomach at the implication behind her words. I turned again to Flint.

"Did the same thing happen to you after the blood binding ceremony with my father?" I asked. "Did you lose touch with your imprint bond to me?"

He said nothing. The hard look in his eyes told me all I needed to know.

He softened his gaze a moment later, but it was like it was rehearsed and not real.

"The bond I have with Azazel is strong," he said. "But I still knew I was imprinted with you, and I wanted to mate with you. We wouldn't be here otherwise."

He said it so... robotically.

The Flint I was speaking to now was a different person from the Flint I knew and loved before the blood binding ceremony.

That Flint loved me and would have given the world to mate with me.

As a demon, I knew how blood binding worked. Flint—and any other shifters bound to my father—would want what my father wanted.

My father wanted Flint and I to mate to show unity. He wanted other shifters to see that this alliance we'd made was built on love, not on threats. Plus, he was curious about what would happen when a shifter mated with a demon.

Flint hadn't told me he loved me since the blood binding ceremony.

Now that he was bound to my father, he'd only wanted to mate with me because my *father* wanted him to mate with me.

The realization made me feel like I was drowning in despair. It hurt to breathe. I tried steadying my breaths, but there wasn't enough air in the room to keep me steady and focused.

"Mara?" Sage asked from overhead. Her voice sounded distant and hazy. "Are you okay?"

No, I wanted to say. *I'm mated to the shadow of a man whose love for me has been overpowered by his bond to my father. How can I ever be okay again?*

But of course I didn't say that. The mate bond was for life. The demon bond... well, as far as I was concerned, that was for life too.

The Flint I'd loved was never coming back. And because we were mated, I'd never fall in love again.

I wished I'd had more time between the blood binding ceremony and the mating ceremony. If I'd had the time, I would have realized how much Flint had changed.

If given the time, I might not have gone through with it.

Thomas needed to know Sage was lost to him. That way, he'd be given the chance I never had. The chance to let her go.

"I'll alert Azazel so he can go to the meeting location tomorrow at noon," Flint decided. "He shouldn't have a problem killing Thomas."

I looked to Sage, assuming she'd have *some* kind of reaction to the thought of the death of this man who loved her. She'd loved him before blood binding with my father. So she had to feel something. Right?

She was completely emotionless.

"If that's what you and Azazel think is best..." she said with a slight pause. "I'll stand by your decision."

"Wait," I said.

Both of them turned to me. Sage's eyes widened, startled. Flint's brow furrowed in worry.

"Yes?" Flint asked, warning in his tone.

I took a deep breath. I needed to get a grip on myself and be the cool, calm demon they expected me to be.

They'd be more likely to listen to me that way.

"Thomas will be no use to us if he's dead," I said, casually glancing at the letter. "Why not use his feelings to get him to join our side?"

The corner of Flint's lips flicked up into a smile. "Fascinating," he said, looking over to Sage. "What are your thoughts, little sister?"

Sage pressed her lips together, as if nervous. She looked from Flint to me, and then back to Flint. "Azazel did say he wants more numbers," she said carefully. "If we can convince Thomas to go through a blood binding ceremony, I only see that as being a good thing."

"Only shifters can blood bind with demons," I

informed them. "But *any* supernatural can enter into a blood oath. My father will ensure the wording of the oath is clear cut enough to have Thomas's loyalty." I smiled, as if relishing in the thought. "He's going to be so pleased to have a vampire on our side. And not just any vampire. A vampire prince."

"He will." Sage nodded, although her eyes were far off. Troubled. "But I'm not sure Thomas would enter into a blood oath with a demon."

"I thought you said he loved you?" I asked.

"He does." She tilted her head, confused. "At least, it appears he does from this letter."

Were her feelings truly so numbed that she couldn't be sure he loved her?

If so, this was definitely the right decision.

"It does," I agreed. "So, here's what I'm thinking we should do..."

They leaned forward to listen, and from there, I told them my plan.

At least, I told them the parts they needed to know.

THOMAS

I arrived at the meeting spot—the Hollywood sign overlooking LA—thirty minutes early. As expected, the hiking trail was crowded with tourists. Perfect.

Despite trusting Sage to come alone, I needed to remain cautious. I couldn't forget that she and the rest of the Montgomery pack were bound to Azazel.

Even if she brought others with her here, they wouldn't risk staging an attack in such a public place. There was too great of a chance of humans getting stuck in the crossfire.

Humans remained rather ignorant to our presence unless they were injured or killed. If that happened, the Vale would swoop in and enact their wrath quickly.

King Alexander was a fairer ruler than the Vale's previous monarch, Queen Laila. But when it came to the laws about keeping the supernatural world hidden from humans, the vampire kingdoms didn't budge, no matter how fair their ruler.

I found a bench underneath a shady tree and sat there as I waited for Sage. While I'd asked her to meet at noon, I was well aware she might hit speed bumps that could make her timing unpredictable. I needed to return to the Devereux mansion before sunset, so I was prepared to wait for Sage until then.

Ten minutes before noon, I smelled the woodsy scent of shifter nearby. My heart leaped, and sure enough, I spotted Sage heading in my direction.

Sunglasses covered her eyes, but she looked more beautiful that ever with her long dark hair blowing behind her as she walked toward me.

I stood to greet her, noticing our imprint bond wasn't flaring up. This was concerning.

Up until now, the bond always flared up when I was close to Sage. Noah had confirmed the same thing happened with him and Raven.

But even though Sage was standing right in front of me, the bond remained as dulled as ever.

I also noticed she wasn't wearing her cloaking ring.

It explained why I was able to catch her scent when she'd gotten near.

"You came." I reached out to take her hands in mine. I needed to touch her—to feel she was real.

She allowed me to take her hands, although they laid limply in mine.

Where was the Sage I knew? The one who used to run for me, wrap her arms around me, and kiss me even at the most inappropriate moments?

"Of course I came." She sounded like she was at a business meeting—not like she was reuniting with someone she loved after being abducted by a greater demon. "I have so much I need to tell you."

"I know what Azazel did to you," I told her, figuring that was what she meant. "You don't have to hide your eyes from me. Once we're back at the Devereux mansion, we'll figure out a way to fix this."

"I'm not going to the Devereux mansion," she said simply.

"The mansion is safe," I assured her. "Their sister Whitney used her Final Spell to create a powerful barrier around it. Azazel won't be able to get to you in there. I promise."

"I understand," she said. "Which is why I won't go there."

I furrowed my eyebrows in confusion. Why would she say such a thing?

I glanced around the area, instantly suspicious. Were there other Montgomery pack members in the area, or even Azazel himself? Had they discovered my letter? Had they forced Sage to come here anyway and followed her here?

It would explain why she was acting so strange and distant. She was trying to warn me.

I tried to tune into the imprint bond, wanting to ask her privately if we were safe to speak freely. But I couldn't tap into it. It was there, but at the same time, it was impossible to hold onto.

My frustration grew as my attempts failed, until I eventually gave up.

Luckily, there were other ways to communicate with her. We didn't have to rely on magic.

I let go of one of her hands and reached for my cell phone in my pocket. Upon touching it, I used my ability to command a message to appear upon the screen.

Did they follow you here? Do we need to make a run for it?

I angled the message toward her so she could read it. Her sunglasses were so dark that the light of the phone reflected on the lenses.

"We're safe," she confirmed. "But I didn't come here to run off with you."

"Oh?" I asked.

"I came here to make you an offer."

I tilted my head, more confused than ever.

The woman in front of me looked and smelled like Sage. But she wasn't *acting* like Sage. And my imprint bond wasn't responding to her the way it should.

It was like I was speaking with a stranger.

"Take off your sunglasses," I told her. "I want to see your eyes."

She reached for her sunglasses and propped them up on her head. Red eyes stared back at me.

I knew the demon bonding ceremony had changed her familiar warm brown eyes to what they were now. But the coldness in them took me by surprise.

"Happy?" She dropped her arms to her sides, not reaching out for me again.

I nodded, words getting stuck in my throat.

I wasn't the type of man to be caught off guard. In the rare times I was, I'd learned it was best to say nothing.

But Sage had come here for a reason. Whatever that reason was, I needed to know.

I was also grateful she'd come at all. Whatever Azazel had done to her had clearly damaged her in ways I hadn't expected. Cassandra had warned me about this. But Sage was strong. I'd help her get through it.

To do that, I needed to figure out exactly what we were facing.

"What's this offer you came to ask?" I finally forced myself to return to the conversation at hand.

"Would you like to sit?" She motioned to the bench I'd been sitting on when I was waiting for her—when I thought I was about to whisk her away to safety at the Devereux mansion.

Perhaps I'd been foolish to think the plan would play out so easily.

I'd thought we might hit some speed bumps. But I hadn't expected this... shadow of whatever Sage had become. I hadn't expected to feel like I was talking to a stranger.

"No," I replied. "Let's remain standing."

"As you wish." She nodded, still as stiff as ever. "In your letter, you said you had eyes on the Montgomery complex. I take it that means you figured out a way to spy on us?"

"Just long enough to see you were there, and to see you playing along with this alliance Flint made with Azazel." Disgust laced my tone as I spoke the greater demon's name. "Playing along was smart. It kept you alive."

She stared at me, her eyes cold. "I wasn't 'playing along' with anything," she said. "This alliance was meant to be. Flint wouldn't have imprinted on Azazel's daughter otherwise. Now that the Montgomery pack is bonded with Azazel, he's going to keep us safe in the dark times to come. He's our Savior. And Flint made this all happen for us."

"You don't believe that," I said. "You wouldn't be here right now if you did."

"You're wrong," she said. "I came here today because I want you to join us."

I heard her speak, but I couldn't believe the words coming out of her mouth.

I searched her eyes for evidence that she was being coerced—that she was saying this against her will. But she was as serious and calm as ever.

It was like the fire in her soul had been snuffed out completely.

"Azazel won't keep you safe," I said sharply. "He—and all the demons—want the world to themselves. They want all the supernaturals dead."

"He only wants to get rid of those who oppose him and his kind," she said steadily. "Which is exactly why Flint made this alliance. The demons are strong, dangerous enemies. Why fight them when we can join them? When they're offering us their protection?"

"They're not offering you *protection*." I sneered, unable to believe she truly bought what he was selling. "They've turned you into slaves."

"I'm not a slave," she said. "I've pledged loyalty to Azazel. In return, he's pledged loyalty to me. If you do the same—if you make a blood oath to promise your loyalty to him—you'll be protected in the upcoming war. Then the two of us can be together forever." Her eyes softened, and for a moment, I saw a glimmer of the Sage I knew in there. "Isn't that want you want?"

"Is that what *you* want?" I asked in return.

"Of course it is," she said, and my heart fluttered with relief. She *was* still in there. "Your gift with technology will help us so much," she continued. "Azazel will be so pleased with me for bringing you to our side."

She beamed, as if nothing would make her happier than pleasing Azazel.

My hope that she was fighting past the hold he had on her vanished. Whatever magic had been used to create the demon bond was incredibly strong. It had poisoned her down to her soul.

But she couldn't have gone through this willingly. Flint must have forced her somehow. The Sage I knew would never enter into an alliance with Azazel. She would never believe all this crazy stuff she was saying.

She wasn't thinking straight, and she clearly wasn't going to come with me willingly.

But the imprint bond was still there. It was weak, but it was there. Which meant Sage still had to be in there, too.

I was going to have to force her to come with me to the Devereux mansion. Once she was back, the witches would figure out a way to fix whatever Azazel had done to her. They *had* to be able to fix her.

If they couldn't... dread coursed through me at the thought of her staying like this forever.

I wouldn't let myself go there. Because if the Devereux witches couldn't fix Sage, then there had to be other witches who could. Maybe the ones at the Haven, or at one of the other vampire kingdoms. Maybe even at Avalon.

There was always a solution to every problem. And I was going to figure out the solution to this one.

But first, I needed to get Sage to the mansion.

I hated what I needed to do next. It was something I'd vowed to never do to her.

But this was an extreme situation. It required extreme measures.

She'd forgive me. Once the demon bond was broken, she'd understand why I'd done it.

And so I stared straight into her strange red eyes,

readying myself to compel her. "You're going to come with me to the Devereux mansion and stay by my side until we break this spell Azazel has placed on you," I said, pushing magic into my voice as I spoke. "From now until the time the spell is broken, you won't make any attempts to reach out to anyone for help." I reached for her hands, pulling her to come with me. "Now, let's get out of here."

THOMAS

She should have come without hesitation.

Which was why I was unprepared when she pulled out of my grip and stepped back.

I reached for her again with my full strength. She kicked and twisted her body to try getting out of my grip. But I was stronger than her. Plus, I'd helped train her, so I was prepared for her every move.

We remained off to the side of the path as we fought, not coming into contact with any humans. As long as the humans remained untouched, they'd remain ignorant to our fighting.

Once I had Sage locked in position, I looked down into her eyes again and repeated my command.

Suddenly, a woman burst forth from the crowd of humans and pulled Sage out of my grip. As she did it, she swiftly slipped something into my pocket. Then she placed herself between Sage and me, guarding us from one another.

I recognized the petite blonde instantly from the drone footage. She was the demon who had mated with Flint.

Azazel's daughter.

I reached into my pocket, ready to expose whatever she'd put in there. It was a piece of paper. Some sort of note.

She looked at me with tortured red eyes—eyes that begged me to listen to her. Her eyes were more human than any demon eyes I'd ever seen. Sage's included.

Not yet, she mouthed, remaining in front of Sage so Sage couldn't see. *Later*.

It almost seemed like she was trying to help me.

Why would a demon be trying to help me? Especially Azazel's daughter?

I didn't know, but for now that paper wasn't going anywhere.

So I pulled my hand out of my pocket, not taking the paper with it. I'd look at it later. Now, I needed to focus on getting Sage away from these monsters.

"Do you really think we would have been so careless as to allow Sage to come out to meet you without protection from your mind control?" Azazel's daughter asked.

"You're wearing wormwood," I realized, speaking to Sage and not to the demon.

"Wrong." Sage smiled.

"Then how did you resist the compulsion?" I was a vampire prince and Sage was the beta of the Montgomery pack. My magic trumped hers. She only could have resisted it by wearing wormwood.

"I told you—Azazel's protecting me," she said proudly. "His magic is stronger than yours. As is Mara's." She motioned to Azazel's daughter, whose name was apparently Mara.

"We didn't come here to fight." Mara held her hands up like she was declaring peace and backed up to stand next to Sage. "We only want to talk."

"I already tried talking to him," Sage said. "He doesn't appreciate what we're offering. And if I can't get through to him when I'm imprinted to him, I doubt he'll change his mind."

Mara's gaze flickered between Sage and me when Sage mentioned our imprint bond. The demon looked utterly defeated.

But then she wiped her expression clean, looking every bit as detached as Sage.

"You know him best, so I trust your judgment," she

said. "Let's return to the compound. We shouldn't waste any more time here."

"We're just going to leave him here?" Sage looked both shocked and appalled.

"What else do you propose we do?" Mara asked. "Kill him?"

The Sage I knew would have been horrified at the thought.

This Sage watched me coolly, as if thoroughly assessing the situation.

"Is that what Azazel would want us to do?" she finally asked.

"You wouldn't." I stepped forward to reach for her again, but the disgusted look on her face stopped me in my tracks. "We're *imprinted*. That has to mean something for you."

"I already told you." Mara studied me with each word she spoke. "My father's magic is strong. It's stronger than your power of compulsion, and it's stronger than your imprint bond with Sage. Her allegiance is to us now. Not with you. The sooner you understand that, the easier this will be."

Sage just stood there beside her, saying nothing to go against the demon's words.

I didn't want to believe it.

But I also wasn't one to deny what was right in front

of my eyes.

"However, given your imprint bond with Sage, I don't think my father would want you dead," Mara continued. "At least not yet. Because you're not going to give up on her. Are you?"

"Never," I said, since I knew Sage well enough to know she'd been forced or coerced into bonding with Azazel.

"See?" Mara turned to Sage and smiled. "It took some time for Flint to come around as well. And look how that turned out."

I wanted to point out that I was never going to "come around" to making a blood oath with Azazel.

But I held my tongue.

Because I suspected that in some sort of twisted way, Mara was trying to help me.

Of course, I couldn't be sure until reading the note. But if Sage thought I was considering her offer, it would be easier to rescue her once I figured out how to break the bond with Azazel.

"This is a lot to take in, in such a short amount of time," I said, looking at Sage's empty eyes when I spoke. "I'll consider your offer. But I need time to mull it over first."

Sage crossed her arms over her chest, not looking

pleased. "Will Azazel be satisfied with that response?" she asked Mara.

"Given that it took Flint a few days to agree to an alliance, I believe so," Mara replied. "My father understands that your kind struggles with making decisions at the same quick pace we can. You'll find he's rather reasonable when it comes to matters like this."

If Sage was offended by the obvious insult to her species, she didn't show it.

"Fine," she said, turning back to me. "If you decide to accept, you know how to reach me. Until then, don't send me any more letters. Or anything else, for that matter. I have my alliance and my pack now. If you don't want to join us, you have nothing more to say to me."

She turned around to leave, Mara following at her side.

Sage didn't look back at me once. But Mara did. And as strange as it was, the demon appeared to truly sympathize with my present situation.

My heart had been reduced to a dark, empty cave in my chest. What had the world come to, that a *demon* was behaving more empathetically than the love of my life?

Once they were out of sight, I reached into my pocket, took out the note, and unfolded it. The loopy, flawless handwriting was unfamiliar, and a far cry from Sage's messy scrawl.

I glanced to the bottom to see who it was from.

Mara.

Curious, I sat back down on the bench to read it.

Thomas,

You have no reason to trust me. But I hope you'll listen anyway. And I don't have much time alone to write this, so I need to keep it brief.

A few months after returning to Earth, I met Flint and imprinted on him. It was supposed to be impossible for a shifter to imprint outside of the species, although I've since learned of Sage's imprinting on you and of Noah's imprinting on a human.

When my father—the greater demon Azazel—learned of this imprint, he said he would only allow Flint and I to mate if the Montgomery pack aligned with him through a blood binding ceremony.

Flint and the Montgomery pack, including Sage, went through with the ceremony. Afterward, as my father promised, he allowed Flint and I to mate.

I knew something had changed with Flint immediately following the blood binding ceremony. But it was only after the mating was complete that I realized he was no longer the man I loved.

My father's magic is strong. It supersedes the magic that ties Flint and I together.

Flint is devoted to my father now—not to me.

The mating changed me as well, but not in a way I ever expected. I feel things I didn't before. I care about things I didn't before. Which is why I brought Sage to meet with you today. I wanted you to see the effect of the blood binding yourself.

Sage is no longer the woman you imprinted on. Her soul is lost to you. It belongs to my father now.

However, I promise she's safe with us. Of that, you have my word.

Don't make the same mistake I did. Leave her now, while you still have the chance.

Maybe you'll find love again someday. But if you mate with Sage, you'll end up like me—cursed to forever love someone who's unable to love you back. And I wouldn't wish that upon my greatest enemy.

Don't reach out again. If you do, I assure you won't be dealt with kindly.

Sincerely,

Mara

I re-read the letter a few times, unsure what to make of it. I didn't want to believe it could true.

I also couldn't deny what I'd just seen in front of my eyes.

Sage was no longer the person she once was.

But I wouldn't give up on her.

Mara clearly didn't know me. If she did, she'd know I'd never give up on anyone I loved.

However, I couldn't help Sage on my own.

Which meant it was time to come clean to the others about everything I'd been up to these past two days, so we could work together to figure out how to break that blood binding spell ourselves.

NOAH

J sat through breakfast, stunned as I listened to what Thomas had been up to these past two days.

I wasn't surprised he'd contacted Sage and met up with her. I probably would have done the same thing in his shoes. And if he'd succeeded in bringing her back here safely, I would have been grateful.

But he *hadn't* succeeded. And it was because of the same reason I'd suspected when I'd decided it made the most sense to save Raven first.

Sage had been changed in a way we didn't understand, and she wasn't going to leave her pack willingly. The only way to save her was to break the blood bond. And it was going to take us longer to figure out how to do that than it would take us to rescue Raven.

As tempting as it was to rub in the fact that I was right, I didn't. Because I couldn't imagine what Thomas was going through. I hated being away from Raven, but at least I knew where she was. At least I knew she was still *Raven*.

Thomas finished reading Mara's note aloud, and then looked around the table for our reactions.

"This has to be a trick." Bella was the first to react. "Demons don't care about anyone outside of their species. I don't even think they care about most others *in* their species. They don't have consciences."

"She's right," Cassandra added. "A demon wouldn't help you. Mara must be lying."

Thomas's eyes widened with hope. "Which means Sage is still in there," he said.

"I don't know." I didn't want to be the bearer of bad news, but it needed to be said. Everyone turned to me, and I continued, "We both know Sage. If she didn't mean what she was saying, she would have dropped a hint. Something only the two of you would understand. But you said she didn't do or say anything to show she was going along with this against her will."

"No." Thomas's expression hardened again. "She didn't."

"And Mara said she changed after mating with Flint."

"You heard the letter." He motioned to where it now lay on the table. "She said she feels things and cares about things she didn't before."

An idea started forming in my head—a crazy one, but one that also made a strange amount of sense. "You said demons don't have consciences," I said, focusing on Bella and the other witches at the table. "But we all have consciences."

"Of course we do." Bella motioned to all of us right there. "But demons don't. They're the only creatures in the world without consciences. They were locked into Hell because of how dangerous that makes them. Angels are their exact opposite. Their consciences are so strong that they can't bear to be on Earth. It literally hurts their soul to be around the pain and suffering that exists here, which is why they stay in Heaven."

"Interesting." I immediately thought about Annika—how she'd remained in Avalon since becoming the Earth Angel—but quickly refocused to the topic at hand. "And Mara said she changed after mating. It sounds like she somehow gained a conscience."

"That's not possible." Amber's eyes narrowed. "Demons are empty, evil creatures. It's why they belong on Hell and not on Earth."

"But a demon has never mated with a shifter before,"

I said. "And when shifters mate, we give a piece of our soul to our mate and they give a piece of theirs in return." It was why we mated for life. It was impossible to fall in love with another person after having a piece of your mate's soul fused into yours.

"So Mara carries a piece of Flint's soul," Cassandra realized. "But she's a demon. Piece of Flint's soul or not, the core of who she is can't be changed."

"That's not entirely true," I said, and the attention in the room once more flickered to me. "You all know about dyads. Right?"

"Dyads are shifters who can shift into more than one animal form," Thomas answered swiftly.

"Yes." I nodded. "When shifters are born, we can only shift into one animal form. Wolf, coyote, mountain lion, tiger... whatever the apex predator usually is of the local area. Normally, we imprint with shifters who share that same animal form. But sometimes, we'll imprint with a shifter who has a different animal form. When two shifters with different animal forms mate, they're then able to shift into two forms —their original form, and the form of their mate. The mating changes who they are, both outwardly and inwardly."

"But Mara can't shift into a wolf," Bella pointed out.

"Maybe she can." I shrugged. "We don't know what

she can do. This is the first time a non-shifter has mated with a shifter."

"That we know of," Thomas added.

"This is insane." Amber rubbed her index finger against one of her temples, as if just the thought of this was stressing her out. "This is a *demon* we're talking about. They're sociopaths. It's why they were locked in Hell. It's why we want to kill the ones on Earth now."

"Well, from what Mara wrote in the letter, she either gained a conscious from mating with Flint or she's lying," Thomas said. "But the most important thing for us to focus on is learning more about the demon binding so we can fix what happened to Sage."

"We've already looked through every book in our library," Bella said. "Like I've told you, the only witches who know how to reverse what happened to Sage are the ones in the family that created the spell. It would have to be an old dark magic family. Those families tend to be reclusive. We can't exactly call them up and ask them to spill their deepest family secrets."

I blinked a few times, feeling like an idiot.

Because she was right that she'd already told us this.

Right afterward, Raven had communicated with me through the imprint bond to give me her coordinates. I'd been so excited about locating Raven again that I hadn't thought about the conversation since.

Now that we were discussing it again, it was ridiculously obvious.

Because the answer had been in front of my face since the night we'd spied on Flint and Mara's mating ceremony.

NOAH

"Azazel and the Montgomery pack have to be working closely with this ancient, dark witch family to have gone through the blood binding ceremony," I said. "So it would make sense for one of those witches to be at the mating ceremony too. And there was one woman there without red eyes who isn't part of the pack..." I dropped what I was eating and rushed to the office.

Everyone else followed at my heels.

"Bring up the footage from Flint and Mara's mating ceremony," I told Thomas. "A part that shows the faces of everyone there."

The recording showed up on the big screen television in seconds. He paused on a spot that showed a view of all the attendees.

I stepped forward and pointed at a woman with long, jet-black hair wearing a white dress that hung to the floor. "That's her," I said.

Thomas zoomed in on the woman. The image was pixelated, but her pale, sallow features now filled the screen.

"Do any of you recognize her?" I asked the witches.

"Like I said, the ancient families are reclusive," Bella said. "They don't live in the middle of Beverly Hills like we do."

"You're not an old family?" I'd always assumed they were because they were so powerful.

"No." Amber shook her head, her eyes bugged out in horror. "We have as much power as they do, but we were bred overtime to be this way. The ancient families remain so powerful because… well, they keep their breeding in the family."

"Gross." I crinkled my nose in disgust. "So you have no idea which family this woman might be from?"

"We've never seen her before." Bella tilted her head, studying the image. "But she has the look of a Foster witch, doesn't she?" The question was directed to the other witches in the room—not to Thomas or me. "She looks like the pictures of them I've seen in books."

"Hair black as tar and skin white as snow." Amber's lips formed into an O of surprise as she traced her index finger along the woman's features on the screen. Then she dropped her hand down to her side and turned back to face us, her eyes serious. "But the Foster witches were all killed during the Great War. They created the spell to lock Geneva into the ring, but they were killed in battle by Nephilim before they could perform the spell themselves."

"A spell so strong it required their Final Spells to work." Bella crossed her arms and smirked. "Convenient."

"What are you saying?" Amber asked.

"What if they weren't actually killed in the Great War?" she replied. "What if they created the spell, and then faked their deaths so another witch circle could sacrifice themselves to stop Geneva?"

"That's twisted," Cassandra said.

"The Foster witches were notorious for being twisted," Bella said.

I didn't comment on that, since I was already a few steps ahead after hearing them mention Geneva. "Could the Foster witches have also created a cavern that kills most people who enter?" I asked. "And could they have placed weapons in that cavern? Weapons connected to the souls of demons?"

"You're talking about the Crystal Cavern," Cassandra said. "Aren't you?"

"Yes," I answered.

"They could have," Bella mused. "But they only would have done that if they knew that sometime in the future, someone would enter the cavern and draw blood with one of the weapons to release a demon soul trapped inside. You're talking about over a century of deception. Which yes, the Foster witches are definitely capable of."

Amber rolled her eyes. "One grainy photo, and you're already talking about the Foster witches like they're still alive," she said.

"You're the one who pointed out that the witch at the mating ceremony looks *exactly* like the old pictures of the Foster witches," Bella said. "It's not far-fetched to think their descendants would look similar, given their inbreeding."

The two witches stared at each other, neither looking like they were going to back down.

"Can you retrieve these books you're talking about?" Thomas asked. "It'll help if we can see photos of the Foster witches ourselves."

Evie and Doreen jumped up to leave the room and fetch the books. They weren't nearly as chatty as their sisters, so I had a feeling they were itching to get a break from our constant strategizing and planning.

They returned a few minutes later. Each of them held two heavy, dusty tomes.

Thomas raised an eyebrow. "Is there any reason why you haven't digitized this yet?" he asked.

"Magic is our specialty," Evie said as she and Doreen dropped the books down on the desk. "Not technology."

"Once this is all over, perhaps I can be of some assistance," Thomas offered.

"Just like that?" Bella looked at him suspiciously. "No catch?"

"You're already helping me," he said. "And it seems like you'll continue to do so. It's the least I can do in return."

As they spoke, Evie was already searching through one of the books. She flipped rapidly through the contents. Finally, she settled on a page and called us over to look.

It was a family portrait of five Foster witches, dated 1925. Four years before the Great War. It was a typical family of five, with a mother, father, and three children. All with black hair and pale skin. The husband and wife looked like they could be brother and sister. From what the Devereux's had said about inbreeding in the ancient families, they possibly were.

I shuddered at the thought. No wonder they all looked so miserable in the photo.

Sure enough, the witches in the portrait had a similar look to the one who'd attended Flint and Mara's mating ceremony. The woman at the ceremony was in her twenties—younger than the mother in the portrait and older than the children. But it was like looking at a picture of what she would look like in twenty years, or what she would have looked like as a child. The resemblance was uncanny.

Bella looked back and forth between the photo in the book and the one on the screen. "If that woman at the ceremony isn't a Foster witch, then I'll never drink another martini again," she said.

"Don't make promises you can't keep." Amber was trying to joke, but concern was rising in her tone.

Hope spread through my chest at the realization that we were onto something. "It sounds like you all have more research to do regarding the Foster witches," I said. "In the meantime, we don't know what the demons have planned for Raven—and all those other humans— in that bunker. So it's time we get them out of there before we find out."

RAVEN

*F*ive days.

That was my first thought when the bugle woke me up that morning.

Each day that passed, I wondered if it would finally be the day Noah broke in and rescued me. I continued to message him every day, telling him not just my location and details about the bunker, but other facts about day-to-day life here. I wanted to give him anything that might prove helpful.

He had yet to reply to my messages. But Donna had promised me he was receiving them. Her Magic 8-Ball gift didn't lie.

Even if she *were* lying, Jessica would be able to detect it.

I wished I knew why he wasn't replying. Unfortunately, no one in the bunker had a gift that could help me out there. So I'd just have to wait until Noah and I were together again to ask him myself.

In good news, Donna had been able to tell me that my mom was still alive. That and knowing that Noah was receiving my messages were the only things keeping me going right now.

Every muscle in my body hurt as I got out of bed and trudged to breakfast. The workout routine Dr. Foster had given me was brutal, and the demons insisted I follow it exactly.

I was so sore that even sitting down to use the toilet was painful.

Breakfast was the typical fare of oatmeal, fruit, and orange juice. I stirred the oatmeal around and glared at it. I didn't want to eat another bite of oatmeal again in my life. But that wasn't an option right now, so I forced it down. Everyone else in the dining hall did the same.

We were one beaten, depressed group.

As the meal was ending, Marco approached our table.

I looked down at my empty bowl. Hopefully I hadn't done something wrong. All I had left was one piece of fruit and a few sips of orange juice. I was on track to finish my meal with everyone else.

But the demon guard wasn't looking at me. He was looking at Jessica.

"Number thirty-five," Marco addressed Jessica. "The doctor has declared you ready for the next location."

All of the color drained from Jessica's face. "No," she said, holding onto the edges of her seat. "I won't go."

"You'd rather stay here?" Marco chuckled.

"The next location is worse than here," she said hollowly.

"Who told you that?" he asked.

"You did... by never saying otherwise," she said. "You've been lying by omission. Tell me the next location isn't worse than this. Tell me, and I'll know if you're telling the truth."

"You might be able to detect lies." Marco sneered. "But it doesn't stop you from saying them yourself."

"I'm not lying." Jessica raised her voice so everyone in the dining hall could hear. "The next location is worse than here. You're getting us in shape, feeding us well... for what?"

He raised a hand and slapped her hard on the cheek, knocking her out of her chair. The sound of it echoed through the room.

She tumbled onto the ground and stared up at him in terror.

He raised his fist again to do more, and I couldn't

help myself. I was up out of my seat, trying to push him away from her before I could think twice about it.

He slapped me to the ground beside her before I could blink.

"Have a big head because you were traveling with supernaturals before coming here, don't you?" he asked mockingly.

I glared up at him, saying nothing.

"You might have supernatural friends, but they're not here to protect you now." He smiled, and his pointed demonic teeth flashed beneath his glamour. "You're just a human. Forget your place again, and you'll get a lot worse than a slap."

"He's lying," Jessica whispered. "They can't hurt us too much. They need us in good condition for the next location."

"Enough from you." Marco yanked Jessica up from the floor and dragged her toward the door. He stopped a moment before leaving and turned back to face us, holding her firmly in place. "The next location *is* better than here," he said, projecting so everyone in the dining hall could hear him. "But to get there, you need to be useful. So finish your meals. You're going to need it."

To best keep tabs on what was going on in the bunker, we'd adjusted our schedule to Nebraska time instead of California time.

Now I was in the living room with the witches, watching the bunker security cameras as the demon guard slapped Raven to the floor at the end of their breakfast.

Without audio, it was impossible to know what they were saying. But something was happening to the teenage girl Raven had befriended. Raven was trying to stand up for her.

As I watched, I clenched my fists so tightly that my nails dug through my skin.

Not being able to help Raven was killing me. I wished I could communicate with her through the imprint bond like she could with me, but it was impossible. Every time I tried, it was like hitting a brick wall.

I was still staring at the screen, seething about not being able to jump right there and ram my slicer through the demon guard's heart, when Thomas entered the room.

He had his phone in hand. "I just finished talking with Shivani from the Haven," he said. "They're on board with the plan. Once our part is done, I'll give them another call and they'll drop in to help us from there."

I nodded, glad that Shivani wanted to help. She'd been my witch contact at the Haven when I was working to create peace between the wolves and vampires of the Vale. She'd always struck me as reasonable.

At the same time, I never trusted when things worked out *too* smoothly.

Especially since the last time I'd done that, Azazel had abducted Raven and Sage.

"That took less time than expected," I said.

"The Haven is curious about why the demons are so interested in these particular humans," Thomas said. "They see this as an opportunity to gather information that might help us win this war."

"Perfect." Bella rubbed her hands together in anticipation. "When are we heading out?"

"All of the humans will be in the dining hall for lunch for forty-five minutes," I said, since that was the plan—we'd strike when the humans were all together. That only happened during meals. Thanks to the demons' nocturnal schedule, lunch started at midnight. Since Thomas couldn't risk being weakened due to sunlight exposure, it made the most sense for us to strike then. "So we need to start preparing now."

*M*arco was so much stronger than me that fighting against him was futile. But it didn't stop me from trying.

If he was going to drag me out of here kicking and screaming, then so be it.

Turned out he didn't actually have to drag me. We'd barely made it into the hall of the bunker when he picked me up and threw me over his shoulder.

"No!" I screamed, hitting him as hard as I could in the back. He didn't even flinch. "You won't get away with this."

"I have, and I will," he said, tightening his hold around my waist. "Stop screaming. No one's going to hear you. At least, no one who can save you."

I automatically knew he was telling the truth. That

was how my gift worked—someone spoke, and I *knew* if it was a truth or a lie. Knowing was as natural to me as breathing.

He walked to the end of the hall, where there was one door that was bigger than the others. The exit. At least, I'd always assumed it was the exit. I'd never seen anyone enter or exit from it, so there was no way to know for sure.

He only needed to use one arm to hold me up. He used the other to open the door. It led to a staircase, with another big heavy door at the top. He pushed through that door and carried me into the foyer of what looked like a deceptively normal country house. It was hard to see from the angle I was thrown over his shoulder, but I could make out another staircase, and a dining room in front of me.

"Help!" I screamed, figuring it couldn't hurt to try again. "Someone, please help!"

"What didn't you understand about 'no one's going to help you?'" Marco grumbled.

I screamed again and hit him again, mustering up as much force as possible behind the punch. I kicked my legs too, hoping to get him in the face.

He just squeezed me tighter—so tight I could barely breathe, let alone scream.

Cold terror rushed through my veins as he carried me up the stairs.

Was this it? Was he going to kill me?

No, I thought, shaking the thought out of my head. If the demons wanted us dead, we would have already been dead. Why would they have gone through so much trouble to get us healthy and in good physical shape if they were just going to kill us?

"Are you going to kill me?" I asked.

"No," he answered. "I'm not going to kill you."

He was telling the truth.

Okay. This was good.

As long as I was alive, there was still a chance I could get away from all of this. There was still a chance I could get back home and see my parents and brother again.

"Natasha! Dimitri!" Marco called as he walked through the upstairs hall. "One of the humans is ready for you."

One of the doors opened, followed by the other. A woman with unbrushed, dark-blonde hair stood in one, wearing pajamas. A man who looked like her—likely her brother—stood in the other.

"My turn," the woman said in a distinctly Russian accent, looking over at the man in challenge. "You had the last one."

The man eyed me up. "This one looks small," he said to Marco in the same accent as the woman. "Are you sure she's ready?"

"She's young, but she's healthy," Marco said. "The doctor said it's time."

"Why not wait until she's older?" The woman stepped forward and reached for my chin, holding onto my face and studying me. Her skin was surprisingly cold. "She doesn't look a day over fourteen."

"I'm sixteen," I told her, staring straight into her eyes.

Whenever I looked at one of the demons for long enough, I got a glimpse of the true red color of their eyes. But this woman's—Natasha's—light blue eyes remained the same color.

She wasn't a demon.

Hope surged through my chest. Maybe she'd be able to help me.

"Better than fourteen." She gave an approving nod and let go of my face, dropping her arm back to her side.

"Better for what?" I asked.

Marco spoke up before she could answer. "Be careful what you say around this one," he warned. "She's a human lie detector. That's her gift."

Natasha licked her lips, her eyes glimmering with interest. "I'll be sure to keep that in mind," she said.

Marco heaved a sigh and continued forward.

Given my uncomfortable perch over his shoulder, I could only see behind him. But I heard the click as he opened another door. He walked us up another set of stairs, and Natasha and Dimitri followed behind us.

Once we were upstairs, Marco dropped me down onto a bed. It was a twin bed in a sparsely furnished attic. The roof slanted up to meet in the middle, and there were only two small windows—one on each end of the room. Both had the shades drawn.

"I'll leave you to it," Marco said to the siblings. "Let me know once it's done so I can call Lavinia."

Natasha nodded and stood straight, looking at Marco. "Soon he will rise," she said, her tone dark and serious.

"Soon he will rise," Marco repeated in the same mysterious tone.

The demon turned around and left the attic, leaving me alone with Natasha and Dimitri. They both watched me with sharp, hawk-like eyes.

Dread settled into my gut. I wasn't sure why I'd thought there was a chance they might help me. They might not be demons, but they were obviously working with them.

I eyed up the door. Part of me wanted to make a run

for it. But where would I go? According to Kara, we were in the middle of nowhere. Even if I got out of this house, I couldn't outrun the demons. Maybe I could hide from them. But they had a supernatural sense of smell. They'd find me like a bloodhound on a deer.

Trying to get on the good side of these people— Natasha and Dimitri—was my only option. At least they weren't demons.

Maybe they'd have some compassion.

"What are you guys?" I asked them. "Your eyes don't flash red, so I know you're not demons."

"Correct." Natasha circled me like a hawk, looking amused.

Dimitri stood near the door, ready to catch me if I tried to run.

"Are you supernaturals?" I asked.

She walked toward me and placed her hands on my shoulders. Her grip was strong—even if I wanted to run, I could feel I wouldn't be able to. "Enough with the questions." She smiled, fangs extending next to her front teeth. "I'm hungry—and you smell delicious."

I didn't have time to scream before she pushed me down onto the bed and dove at my neck.

There was a short prick of pain when her fangs pierced my skin, and then... a rush of euphoria.

Pleasant tingling overtook my body, starting with the tips of my fingers and toes and traveling up my limbs. It was like she was drugging me. I stared up at the ceiling, unable to move my head to look anywhere else. The cobwebs hanging from the beams looked like a soft, comfortable blanket overhead.

They shimmered as they moved in the draft, and I stared and stared at them until it felt like I'd been staring at them forever.

When was Natasha going to stop drinking?

I wanted to ask, but my mind was muddled and fuzzy. It was like whatever connected my brain to my mouth had stopped working.

So I just lay there, letting her take more and more of my blood. There couldn't be much left for her to drink. How much more blood could I have?

Not enough.

She wasn't going to stop. She was going to drain me dry.

I was never going to see my family again.

What would they think happened to me?

I tried to move my fingers, but it was like my mind was separated from my body. All I could control now were my eyes. But even they felt weighted and heavy. Keeping them open took an energy I no longer had. All I wanted was to go to sleep.

At least I wasn't in pain. Of all ways to die, I supposed this wasn't so bad.

So I let my eyes fall shut, floating and spinning as I sunk down into the darkness until eventually, there was nothing.

NOAH

$\mathcal{T}$homas estimated it would take a maximum of fifteen minutes for us to break into the bunker, and a minimum of five. Breaking in too early—before everyone got settled in the dining hall for lunch—would result in complete pandemonium. Since we had a forty-five minute window to work with, it was better to be slightly late than slightly early.

We gathered in the living room again at ten minutes to Nebraska's midnight, geared up and ready to go.

The television screen was now split into two sections. One side showed views from the cameras inside the bunker. Raven and the others were finishing up their mid-morning workouts. They'd be headed to lunch soon.

The other side showed satellite images of the farmhouse above the bunker. Surrounding the house were cornfields as far as we could see. I'd never seen so much flat land in my life.

"This shouldn't be hard," Cassandra said as she studied the farmhouse. "If we don't land right outside of the house, we'll land somewhere in the fields. It'll be easy to make our way to the house from there."

Thomas and I each needed a witch to teleport us to the bunker, and Cassandra and Bella had been quick to volunteer. Cassandra and Thomas were a duo, so she'd teleport him. The Devereux's hadn't liked the idea of *any* of them leaving the safety of the mansion, but they all agreed that Bella was the best in combat. So they'd agreed it made the most sense for her to accompany me. Especially since she was getting stir-crazy staying inside all day.

The rest of them—Amber, Evie, and Doreen—would stay behind. Amber couldn't leave, since she needed to use her light magic to maintain the boundary spell around the house. So she, Evie, and Doreen were going to keep investigating the Foster witches and see what they could come up with.

"I never thought I'd ever go to Nebraska." Bella took a final look at the satellite imagery on the screen, and then held out a hand for me to take. "You ready?"

"More than you know," I said, since every minute

that passed was a minute closer to reuniting with Raven. "But are you sure you're good in those shoes? It might be hard to run in the corn fields." I eyed up the shoes in question—knee-high boots with a tall pointed heel in the back.

Sage had once used a special word to describe that type of heel. Something that sounded dangerous.

Sage was a skilled fighter, but even *she* didn't fight in shoes like that.

"They're enspelled for maximum comfort." Bella smiled and examined her boots with pride. "Plus, the stilettos double as weapons."

That was the word Sage had used. Stiletto.

Once we were all out of this mess, I'd ask Bella to whip up some magical stilettos for Sage. She'd love them.

"Great." I took Bella's hand and glanced at Thomas and Cassandra to see if they were ready to go as well. They were. "Let's do this."

NOAH

Bella used one hand to hold mine and the other to hold Cassandra's. This way, the four of us would all end up in the same location.

As expected, we landed straight in the middle of a field. But the satellite photos Thomas had shown us must have been old. Because this land wasn't green and bursting with crops.

It was flat, brown, and dead.

One whiff of the surrounding air, and I could smell that no crops had been planted here yet this season. Whoever owned this land didn't care about it, had abandoned it, or had been killed for it.

Since the farmhouse was now occupied by demons, I suspected the latter.

Once verifying that we'd all arrived in one piece, I

turned around to get my bearings. The farmhouse was a dot out on the horizon. It looked like the witches had been a few miles off.

It shouldn't take us more than a minute or two to cover this distance. Of course, I'd be faster if I shifted into wolf form. But we didn't know if there were any demons guarding the outside of the house. I didn't smell any nearby, but they could be wearing cloaking rings. I'd need to stay in human form so I could grab my slicer in a moment's notice, just in case.

"Not too bad for the first time here," Bella said, gazing out at the house in the distance.

Thomas glanced down at his watch. "Their lunch is starting in a few minutes," he said. "Let's go."

He didn't need to say it twice. I was immediately running through the field, the house getting closer by the second. The others were right on my heels.

I was halfway there when the ground rumbled and shook beneath my feet, knocking me off-balance. And the shaking didn't stop. It got stronger and stronger, until all I could do was dig my fingers into the dirt and brace myself on all fours.

I glanced behind to make sure the others were okay. They were, although they were all on the ground in similar positions.

Then I heard an audible rip. I focused ahead again,

just in time to see the ground split open twenty feet ahead of me.

A giant, insect-like monster with a human face emerged from the gap. Its head was as tall as my body, and its tail was like a scorpion's, but larger. Its body was segmented into three main parts—the head, the middle, and the tail. Six spindly legs protruded straight out of the middle section.

Once it was fully above ground, the ground sealed beneath it.

"Cross onto this land and die," the monster said, his deep baritone voice echoing through the field. His breath reeked of rot and decay, which I supposed made sense for a creature that had spent who knows how long buried in the dirt.

"We intend to cross." I looked straight into its eyes, hoping it respected a solid stare like a shifter would. "And we *don't* intend to die."

"Too late." He cackled. "You already crossed. Now, you die."

Before I could comprehend what was happening, the creature swung his spiky tail out at me.

I jumped out of its way at the same time as I reached for my slicer.

His tail hit exactly where I'd been standing before, the tip of it lodging into the dirt.

So much for that stare. But with my slicer out, I was ready to fight. A glance over at Thomas—who was wielding the longsword he'd brought with him like a pro —showed he was ready as well.

I gave the vampire a single nod, and the two of us attacked.

The monster's front two legs seemed like a good place to start. Remove the legs, and it would be immobilized.

I ran to one leg, and Thomas must have understood my plan, because he ran to the other.

I expected the leg to be easy to cut through, like a normal limb. But my dagger clanged against it, a sound of metal on metal echoing through the air.

This creature's legs were as strong and solid as a sword.

It used its legs like swords, too. On instinct, I met each of its attacks with one of my own, defending myself.

Thomas did the same. He took three legs, and I took the other three. Hopefully we could divide and conquer.

Except the creature had no problem keeping up. It wasn't even tiring.

In the meantime, Cassandra was shooting arrows at the creature from a distance. It used its tail to ward off most of them. The few that landed in its body didn't bother it at all.

The arrows that landed on the ground whooshed back into Cassandra's quiver, ready to be used again.

That was a pretty neat spell. I'd have to ask her about it later.

The monster finally grunted when an arrow embedded itself into one of its eyes. So Cassandra switched up her aim to try for the eyes. A few got close, but she had yet to get another into the target.

She was never going to take down the monster like this.

There had to be another way.

As I continued fending off the legs, I sized the creature up to figure out another method of attack.

The two thin parts holding the three sections of its body together looked the weakest. Snap off the head or abdomen, and maybe the creature would be toast.

I just needed a break in fighting off these three legs so I could have a chance to see if my idea worked.

Hopefully Cassandra would hit an eye again soon to give me the precious few seconds I needed.

But it wasn't Cassandra who got me those seconds. It was Bella.

The Devereux witch launched a potion pod straight

at the monster's nose. The pod collided with its target and exploded into a dark blue mist.

The creature faltered.

I'd never seen dark blue potion before, so I had no idea what it was for. Knowing Bella, it was some kind of secret dark magic.

But whatever the potion was, it gave me the seconds I needed to enact my plan.

I launched myself into the air in an attempt to dismember the middle section from the abdomen. I was just about there when I saw something descending from the corner of my eye—the creature's tail.

I didn't know what a sting from this beast would do to me, and I didn't want to find out. So I aborted the mission, using my knife against the tail instead of slashing it through the thin skin between its middle section and abdomen.

Its tail was just as hard as its legs. The force of my knife pushed the dangerous stinger away from me, but it also pushed me back onto the ground.

I rolled and recovered just in time to get out of the way as the tail went in for another blow.

Bella launched three potion pods in a row at the creature—one at each of its sections. The blue mist exploded again, and this time, the creature didn't just falter.

It froze entirely.

"Try again!" she yelled. "Both of you."

Thomas jumped up for the spot between the head and the middle, and I jumped back to where I'd gone before. Between the middle and the abdomen.

This time, I hit my mark.

My dagger slid through the thin membrane holding the two parts together.

Without the middle part holding it up, the abdomen fell onto the ground. A glance to my side showed that the head was also on the ground. Thomas had been successful too.

Without the head or abdomen attached any longer, the creature's legs shuddered and crumpled inward. The lone middle section collapsed onto the ground.

Dirt poofed out around it. One of the legs gave a final twitch, and then went still.

"Is it dead?" Cassandra asked. She had an arrow poised and ready to launch straight at its unblinking eye, just in case.

I wasn't sure any of us knew the answer. We were all ready with our weapons ourselves.

Seconds later, all three separated sections of the monster disintegrated into dirt. It blended into the rest of the dirt in the field, as if the creature had never been there at all.

If there was one thing I'd learned from the past few weeks of demon hunting, it was that when something disintegrated, it was pretty darn dead. So I relaxed, although I kept my slicer out and ready.

"What the hell was that thing?" I asked, looking at the others for answers.

"That *thing* was one of Abaddon's Locusts," Thomas said as he sheathed his sword. "A monster that serves the demons."

"Right," I said, although I'd never heard of Abaddon *or* his locusts. "Why didn't you see it when you tapped into the satellites?"

"Satellites only detect what's above ground—not below it," he said. "I'm a technopath. I don't have X-ray vision."

His point was fair, so I nodded and slid my dagger back inside my jacket.

"I have a better question," Cassandra said, completely focused on Bella.

"What's that?" Bella smiled, like she not only knew what was coming, but welcomed it.

"Why did you have complacent potion?"

"I abduct some of the most dangerous human criminals in the world to kill them for my potions and spells," she said. "Having complacent potion on hand helps the abducting part go smoother than it would otherwise."

Cassandra pressed her lips into a firm line. "Complacent potion is illegal," she said simply.

"It's only illegal if you get caught." Bella shrugged.

"The law doesn't work like that." Cassandra's eyes were bugging out, like she was afraid of getting arrested in a moment's notice.

I was on Bella's side here. Whatever she'd done had saved us.

But the witches could work it out later. *After* we saved Raven and the other humans from that bunker.

"The complacent potion just saved your asses," Bella said. "You should be thanking me—not chastising me."

"How much more do you have left?" I asked.

"None," she said. "That monster was huge. It took four times a normal dose just to placate him for the time it did."

There went any possibility of using it against the demons. Oh well. Complacent potion hadn't been in our plan to begin with.

We could handle breaking into the bunker just fine on our own.

$\mathcal{W}$e whizzed past an abandoned barn and stopped in front of the farmhouse.

It was a simple dwelling, two stories tall with white wood paneling. From the outside, there were no signs that an elaborate bunker existed directly beneath it.

It also didn't seem like there was a magical barrier around the house. That was a relief, but not a surprise.

It took a strong light witch to cast and hold a magical barrier. The chance of a witch like that working with the demons was slim to none.

Back at the Devereux mansion, Cassandra had promised us that a secret spell passed down through generations of her family would allow her to get us through any magical barrier. But I was glad she didn't have to use it.

It was best for the witches to save all their energy for fighting the demons.

Thanks to Thomas, we knew the only security cameras in this area were in the bunker—not inside or outside the house. We also knew that except for when a catering truck arrived at six each morning, no one entered or left the house. The blinds were closed at all times, as if the place was abandoned.

We all wore cloaking rings to cover our scents. Now, we all formed a circle and Bella muttered a string of words in Latin. A sound barrier spell.

She'd killed one of the criminals in the dungeon and had a vial of his blood in her weapons belt specifically for this moment. As she spoke the spell, a tingle rushed through my body, like I'd been zapped.

"It's done," she said, unclasping her hands from ours and lowering them to her sides.

Because we were all holding on to each other when she'd cast the spell, we could still hear each other. But no one else would be able to hear us.

There was one final step to our master plan—invisibility potion.

Now that we were right outside the house, we each reached for the vial we'd brought with us. Amber had made it in the same batch, so that after taking it, we'd still be able to see each other.

We uncapped our vials, clinked them together in a toast, and downed the contents. It buzzed through my body as it took hold.

Within seconds, all four of us had the hazy, transparent look of ghosts.

Without the demons being able to smell, hear, or see us, we'd be undetectable. They wouldn't know what had hit them until they were dead.

We probably should have taken the invisibility potion *before* teleporting over here. Maybe then the fight against Abaddon's Locust would have been easier.

But the potion only lasted for so long. We had no clue how close the witches would get us to the farmhouse, and sending them to scout ahead of time would have been unnecessarily risky. So the plan had been to wait to take it until reaching the farmhouse.

Lesson learned.

Now that we were undetectable, I led the others up the steps to the front porch and opened the front door. It creaked when it moved, alerting anyone inside that someone was here.

Immediately upon walking inside the foyer, I was blasted with the distinguishable metallic scent of vampire. It wasn't just a leftover aroma. The vampire was in the house, now.

There was a staircase straight ahead and two rooms

to the side—a dining room and living room. Both of the rooms were empty.

Thomas was the last of us in. Right after he clicked the front door shut, a vampire turned the corner to investigate.

She held up duel daggers as she examined the room. She was short and thin, with dishwasher blonde hair and cunning eyes. Of course, she couldn't see or smell us, and we all stood in place so we didn't risk setting off a creaky floorboard. As long as she didn't walk straight into one of us, she wouldn't know we were here.

"Who's there?" another vampire called from the other room—a male. He had a strange accent I couldn't place.

"No one," she said in a matching accent, although she still looked around suspiciously. "It must have been the wind."

She didn't sound like she believed it.

But she didn't have time to speculate further, because I whipped out my slicer and rammed it through her heart.

She collapsed to the floor, dead.

I would have taken one of her weapons and given the other to another our group. But while our weapons were all invisible since we'd had them on us while drinking the invisibility potion, her weapons were visible. Holding onto them would ruin our element of surprise.

"Natasha?" the man asked, sounding worried. "Is everything okay?"

Not getting a response, he came around the same corner as Natasha. He was short and thin, with similar dishwater blond hair. They were likely siblings.

His eyes widened when he saw his sister crumpled on the floor. He ran to her and repeated her name, rolling her over to see the hole my dagger had left in her chest.

Before he could process Natasha's death, Bella whipped out her longsword and sliced it clean through his neck.

His head clunked to the ground beside him, his body falling down on top of his sister's corpse.

The silence of death descended upon the room.

"Their eyes weren't red," Cassandra said softly. "We were only going to kill the demons or anyone working with them. We don't know why these vampires were here..." She stared down at the bodies, clearly traumatized.

"They were up here where they could leave freely. They weren't locked in the bunker," I said. "They might not have been blood bound, but they were working with the demons." I leaned down and wiped my slicer on the guy's shirt to get Natasha's blood off of it. The blood wasn't invisible, and a floating bit of blood in the shape of a dagger would be a clear giveaway that we were walking around after drinking invisibility potion.

Bella did the same with her longsword.

"We can't know that for sure," Cassandra said.

"Maybe not," Thomas said. "But Noah's right that they weren't being kept here involuntarily. Letting them live would have put our entire plan at risk. And given that we're untraceable, we couldn't exactly wait for them to strike first. Killing them was the only logical choice."

"I guess." Cassandra shrugged, although she kept looking at the dead vampire siblings.

I didn't like killing them either. But if we'd let them live, they would have been able to alert the demons that we were coming.

I wouldn't let *anyone* stop me from saving Raven. I'd come too far to fail now.

Bella glanced down at her watch. "They're already ten minutes into lunch," she said. "We need to find the entrance to the bunker."

"No problem." Thomas reached for the nearest light switch.

Apparently, just touching something electronic in

the house gave him a picture in his mind of the entire electric system. It allowed him to control the system too.

Along with finding the entrance to the bunker, this was when he was going shut off the security cameras and make it look like they were showing what he'd recorded during lunch yesterday. That way, the demons wouldn't see doors opening seemingly by themselves— and anyone watching from outside wouldn't know about the break-in while they could still stop it.

Thomas stared straight ahead, his eyes glazed over for a few seconds. Then he regained focus and lowered his hand from the switch. "Done," he said, heading toward the stairs. "Follow me."

We didn't have to go far before he stopped in front of a plain door on the side of the stairs and opened it.

Behind it was another door. This one was sleek and metallic, with a big clunky box right at eye level.

And the moment the first door was fully open, a red laser beam shot out of the box.

NOAH

*T*homas moved out of the way and held his arm out, stopping any of us from stepping into the laser's path.

"It's a retinal scanner," he said. "It won't hurt anyone. But we shouldn't let it scan any of our eyes, since we're not registered in the system."

I glanced over at the two dead vampires on the floor. "Should I go cut one of their eyeballs out?" I asked. "Scratch that—I'll just bring the guy's head over. It'll be less messy."

"No need." Thomas reached below the laser beam and touched the box. The lock clicked open a second later.

I reached for the handle, and sure enough, the door opened.

Behind it was a staircase that led to a basement. Staring down the stairs, my heart raced with excitement. We were so close to Raven. She was going to be okay.

I was the first down the stairs, the others following on my heels. There was another door at the bottom. This one also had a box attached to it, but no laser beams shot out of this one.

On this box was a screen with a keyboard. It looked like a mini computer.

Thomas took one look at the door, recognition filling his gaze. "A keypad entry," he said, stepping toward it. "I've got this." He pressed his hand to the box, just like he'd done to the retinol scan one earlier. This time, he looked concerned.

"What's wrong?" I asked.

If he couldn't break into this door, I'd run it down myself to get to Raven.

"Nothing." He shook the thought away and started tapping at the keys.

"Lucifer," Cassandra said after he pressed the final letter. "Figures the demons would choose *that* as the password."

The lock clicked open, and I made a mental note to ask more about Lucifer later.

Of course, I'd heard stories about Lucifer—he was the first and most dangerous of all the demons. The wolves of the Vale liked to tell scary stories about him to the pups at night. But he'd been locked up deep in the pits of Hell to make sure he'd never return to Earth again. It would take more than a few minutes of a Hell Gate being opened for Lucifer to escape.

But it was pointless to think about now, since Lucifer wasn't here. Raven was. At least, she was close.

I'd think more about Lucifer and the possible implications of the demons using his name as a password once Raven was safe.

Thomas reached for the door's handle, but he didn't open it. "This door leads straight into the hall of the bunker," he said, and I immediately pictured the layout of the bunker in my mind, since we'd been studying it for days through the surveillance cameras. "As we already know, all the doors inside the bunker use fingerprint recognition technology to open. I just overrode the code and took control of the doors. They're all sealed until I choose to open them. Which means it's go time."

"You all know what we're doing." Suddenly it was like I was back in the Vale, preparing the wolves to march into the vampire kingdom.

Before that battle, Marigold—the possessed witch who was leading the wolves—had given one final pep talk to get everyone in the right mental space for what was to come. Now I wanted to give the others one final reminder of our plan, since so much was on the line.

"There's four of us and four demons," I said. "Once we're inside the dining hall, Thomas will seal the door behind us so the demons can't escape. My slicer is the only weapon that can kill the demons, but I can only kill one at a time. Your job is to hold the other demons off—and keep them from hurting the humans—until I reach your demon to kill it. Since we're all undetectable, it should be easy for each of you to get the upper hand until I reach you. Got it?"

"Got it." Bella unsheathed her sword, anticipation flickering in her eyes as she stared at the shining blade. "Let's kill the demons and figure out what they wanted with those humans."

And save Raven, I thought, although I didn't say it out loud. They knew I wanted to save her.

We each had different reasons for wanting to save the humans. All that mattered was that our end goal was the same.

Thomas opened the door, and together, the four of us hurried down the empty hall toward the door that led to the dining hall, ready to fight.

RAVEN

I was in my seat in the dining hall, forcing down the same lunch we got every day. A turkey sandwich on wheat bread, a side salad, and a glass of milk.

The milk was the hardest to force down. I *hated* drinking milk. One of the few good things about being raised vegan was that I was never forced to drink it.

As I ate, I kept glancing at Jessica's empty seat. When Marco took her, she'd looked terrified. And I'd felt so helpless.

Because what Marco had said about me just being a human... he was right. I was trapped here, powerless against the demons.

I hated it.

I was staring at my glass of milk, disillusioned with

the world, when my chest surged with warmth. It was like the imprint bond had lit up inside of me.

Noah.

I sat up and looked around. He wasn't in here. But I knew that feeling in my chest.

He was close.

Suddenly, the doors to the dining hall opened and the warmth of the imprint bond increased.

I whipped my head around, expecting Noah to be standing there with his slicer.

No one was there.

Strange. The doors never opened during mealtimes. Especially not by themselves.

Everyone else looked equally as confused—including the demons.

"There must be some kind of technology glitch," Marco said, strolling toward the open door. "It'll get fixed later. Keep eating your lunch. No one is leaving here until every plate is clean."

He barely got the last word out before a hole formed in his chest. He lurched forward in pain, his mouth open in shock.

As he was frozen there, the door closed shut again.

Then something came out of the hole in his chest. Something in the shape of a dagger... except all that was visible was the blood *around* the dagger.

Once the dagger was out of Marco's chest, he disintegrated on the spot. He left behind a pile of ashes. All that remained were his teeth.

That wasn't just any dagger.

It was the slicer.

Excitement surged through my veins. Noah was here. He was invisible... but he was here.

He also had three enraged demon guards aware of exactly where he was standing, thanks to Marco's blood covering the slicer.

The closest demon to Marco's remains ran toward where Noah was standing. But he was stopped by an invisible force.

Another invisible person.

Suddenly, the other two demons were getting punched, kicked, and sliced at with invisible forces too. They recovered from the blows and were trying to return the attacks on the invisible assaulters, but they were swinging their swords blindly. Their attempts to fight forces they couldn't see were so pathetic it was comical.

At the same time, the other humans were getting up from their seats, running toward the door.

Harry pressed a finger against the scanner, but it didn't let him through. He cursed and kicked at the door. It didn't budge.

Dr. Foster also ran to the door, but it didn't open for him, either.

The place was a madhouse of humans running around like chickens with their heads cut off and demons unsuccessfully fighting invisible foes.

The only invisible attacker I could locate was Noah, because he was holding the blood coated slicer and because our imprint bond pulled me in his direction. He ran over to the nearest demon and ran the slicer straight through its back.

The demon cried out and arched back, his features twisted in pain.

He was a pile of ashes and teeth a moment later.

I jumped up in victory. But it didn't last long. Because there were two more demons left still alive.

The one on the opposite side of the room ran toward the nearest human—Magic 8-Ball Donna. He swung his sword across her middle and split her in two.

Her eyes went wide with shock, then they glazed over. The two pieces separated and fell to the ground. Her intestines hung out of the openings, dripping out blood, milk, and other types of digested food that I didn't want to think about.

Whoever was invisibly fighting that demon ran straight at him and forced his back to the wall.

The demon jammed his sword repeatedly at the empty space in front of him.

Panic filled every inch of my body. Not my own panic—Noah's.

Something was happening to one of the people who had come with him. Something I couldn't see.

I wished I could help. But there was only one thing I could do to help right now, and it certainly wasn't joining in on the fight. That would only get more people killed. Donna was example enough of that.

"We need to get out of the way!" I yelled, making my way toward the door where Harry and Dr. Foster were already standing. "Everyone, come over here!"

I wasn't sure if they were going to listen to me, but they did. Everyone scurried over to me as quickly as they could, gathering in a huge clump near the door.

Now that the area was clear, the bloodied slicer whizzed across the room. Noah was running. He shoved the demon from the side and pushed it to the floor.

Before I could blink, that demon had turned to ashes, too.

But the victory was semi-sweet. Because as the demon turned to ashes, something in front of him shimmered into view. A body sprawled out on the floor.

Cassandra.

The witch had multiple stab wounds in her stomach,

and she was lying in a puddle of her own blood. There was blood everywhere. She was covered in it. Her hands, her clothes... it was even coming out of her mouth. And her eyes were open and unblinking.

Dead.

The invisibility potion must have stopped working upon her death.

Except that it started wearing off on the others as well. Three more people shimmered into view. A woman whose name I didn't know wearing boots that seemed impossible to fight in, Thomas, and of course, Noah.

Noah held the slicer up and stared at the only remaining demon. His cheeks were splattered with blood, his eyes fierce as ever.

He looked super hot and badass.

The woman was standing closest to the demon, and she jammed her stiletto into his chest. She knocked the wind out of him, giving Noah the perfect opportunity to run at him with the slicer.

The slicer pierced the demon's heart, and he disintegrated to ashes.

Now that all the demons were dead, I ran toward Noah. I threw my arms around him, he picked me right off the ground, and we were a tangle of limbs holding onto each other as he pressed his lips to mine. It felt like we were the only two people in the room, and we kissed each other with as much passion as ever.

"You came," I said once he set me back down.

"Of course I did." His eyes darkened, like he couldn't imagine *not* coming. "I'd never leave you here. You know that, right?"

"You never answered back." I lowered my gaze, feeling foolish. I sounded like a girl upset that her crush never texted her back.

He reached for my chin and lifted it, forcing my eyes to meet his. "I tried," he said. "You have no idea how hard I tried. But tapping into the imprint bond across such a far distance is impossible. You shouldn't have been able to get that message through to me. But you did. Somehow, you did."

He looked at me, as if I had the answer. But I didn't.

"I'm new to this whole imprinting thing. I didn't know what was supposed to be possible or not," I said. "All I'd knew was that I needed to tell you where I was. I couldn't get out of here myself... but I knew you'd think of something. And look—I was right."

"So you pushed past the limits of the imprint bond through sheer stubbornness." He chuckled, watching me with pure admiration. "You're one determined human, Raven Danvers. And I'm so lucky that you're *my* deter-mined human."

"Anyone would have done the same in my situation," I said with a shrug, although I couldn't help smiling, since him calling me *his* made me happier than I'd ever imagined possible.

"They might have wanted to," he said. "But they wouldn't have been able to. The imprint bond only works when we're in the same room as each other. Like I said, what you did was impossible."

"I've seen a lot these past few weeks that I used to think was impossible," I reminded him. "Apparently, there's no limit to what we can do if we truly set our minds to it."

"I don't know," he said. "Don't get me wrong—you're one of the most determined, stubborn people I've ever met. But even you can't change the laws of nature."

Suddenly, I was reminded about what Jessica had said the other night in the bunker. "Maybe I can," I said. "Maybe that's my gift. Stubbornness. You said yourself that I shouldn't have survived after holding onto the slicer so long. But I did. I can also resist the demons' glamour, I convinced Marco to give me my privacy, and I reached you through the bond when I shouldn't have been able to…" As I thought about it, it made more and more sense.

My mom always told me I was too stubborn for my own good.

It was going to be pretty amusing once I finally told her *that* was my ability.

"Gift?" Noah asked. "What do you mean?"

"It's a long story," I said, realizing just how much I'd learned while we'd been apart. "I've got a lot to catch you up on once we're out of here."

"Yes, you do." Noah held me tighter, like he was afraid of ever letting go.

Then someone else cut in, reminding me we weren't actually the only two people in this room.

"I'm glad you're enjoying your reunion," a woman said. "But before you get too comfortable, we've got a problem to handle here first."

I turned to see who had spoken. It was the woman in the stiletto boots.

She'd pushed Dr. Foster down to his knees and was holding a sword up to his throat.

BELLA

With Raven and Noah involved in their reunion and Thomas grieving over Cassandra's bloodied body, it was up to me to apprehend the elephant in the room—the witch who was trying to blend in with the humans.

He didn't really think that was going to work, did he? Sure, he was older and balding, and male witches never had even half the amount of power as female witches.

But he wasn't walking out of here with a get out of jail free card.

Which was why I'd knocked him down to his knees and held my sword up to his throat.

"Oh, right." Noah looked at him, still holding tightly onto Raven. "The witch."

"We need to figure out what he's doing here and what to do with him," I said.

"That's Dr. Foster," Raven chimed in. "He's the doctor at the bunker. I think the demons are holding something over him, because they've been forcing him to—"

"Foster?" I smirked, cutting her off before she could continue. This was too good to be true. "Of course. I heard the Fosters encouraged their males to go into medicine. It was the only way they considered them useful for anything besides reproduction. The entire Foster circle is working with the demons, aren't they?"

"I'm just a doctor," the old man sputtered. "I have no idea what you're talking about."

"Don't even think about lying." I lowered my voice and leaned in closer to his ear. "We know about the blood binding spell. We've seen the shifters affected by it. That spell has powerful Foster magic written all over it."

"The Foster circle has been dead for centuries." He sounded small and afraid. "Maybe they used to be powerful, but not anymore. I'm all that's left. I was kidnapped with the rest of the humans. I don't know anything more about what's going on here. I swear it."

"Are you willing to make a blood oath on that?" I asked.

"Just let me go. Please," he begged. "I won't tell anyone what happened today. I'll make a blood oath promising I won't tell anyone."

"So you're willing to make a blood oath promising not to tell anyone what happened, but not that you don't know anything about it."

A few seconds passed by in silence. The humans just clung to each other, looking both stunned and terrified.

"I was blackmailed," he finally said. "I didn't get to choose what family I was born into. None of us do. I didn't want anything to do with this. I just wanted a normal life. You have to believe me."

I didn't.

Raven shook her head, not looking like she believed him either. "We could really use Jessica right now," she said.

"Who's Jessica?" I asked.

"One of the other humans who was being kept here. She could tell when people were lying or telling the truth."

I hadn't gotten a chance to introduce myself to Raven yet, but that would come later. Obviously she knew I was on her side. Right now, we had more important things to discuss. "How could she tell?" I asked.

"She was gifted," Raven explained. "We all are." She motioned to the other humans to show what she meant.

"Fascinating." I gazed at the humans with newfound admiration.

Mary—the leader of the Haven—had already agreed to let us to bring these humans to her kingdom. She was just as curious about why the demons had taken them as we were.

She was going to be even more interested once she learned they weren't just normal humans, but gifted ones.

"What do the demons want with all these gifted humans?" I asked. "You know, Dr. Foster. Don't you?"

I didn't expect him to answer—yet. But he didn't need to know that. We'd crack him in time.

"I don't," he said. "Even if I did, I wouldn't tell."

"Well, we're all heading off to the Haven, and you're coming with us." I was able to speak freely about our plans, since Thomas had turned off all recording devices. No need to worry about demons listening in here. "We'll see how long you stick to that story once we're there."

I pulled my sword away from his neck and sheathed it by my side. Dr. Foster was just a simple male witch—he had no chance of getting out of here.

He knew it too, since he made no moves to fight. He just rubbed at his neck, his head hung in defeat.

With my hands now free, I pulled out my cell phone to make a call.

Shivani—our witch contact at the Haven—answered on the first ring. "I take it everything went according to plan?" she asked.

"The demons are all cleared from the bunker," I confirmed. "But it won't be long until someone notices they're gone. We've got one vampire, one shifter, one male witch, and thirty-six gifted humans ready for transport. We need them all out of here, now."

"Gifted humans?" Shivani repeated. "Are you sure?"

"I am."

"We'll send our best witches to retrieve them," she said. "Mary's going to love this."

"Yes." I smiled as I looked at the surprisingly healthy humans around me. "She most certainly will."

Thank you for reading The Angel Gift! I hope you loved this book as much as I loved writing it. If you absolutely *need* to talk about it, hop on over to my Facebook group! I love connecting with my readers on there. Just CLICK HERE or visit www.facebook.com/groups/michellemadow.

Get ready for more magic, romance, and twists in the next book in the series—The Angel Island—releasing December 2018! (They'll *finally* get Avalon in The Angel Island ;)

To receive an email alert from me when The Angel Island is live on Amazon, CLICK HERE or visit www.michellemadow.com/subscribe and sign up for my newsletter.

To receive a Facebook message from me when The Angel Island is live on Amazon, CLICK HERE or visit manychat.com/L2/michellemadow.

If you haven't read the first season of the Dark World Saga yet—The Vampire Wish—I recommend checking it out while you're waiting for The Angel Island. The best part is that the series starts with a FREEBIE, The Vampire Rules!

CLICK HERE or visit michellemadow.com/freevampirerules to grab The Vampire Rules and start reading it now.

To get the freebie, you'll be subscribing to my newsletter. I love connecting with my readers and promise not to spam you. But you're free to unsubscribe at any time.

You can also check out the cover and description for The Vampire Rules below. (You might have to turn the page to see the cover.)

Before he was a vampire prince, he was just Jacen.

As one of the most promising athletes in the country, Jacen has his life all mapped out for himself. Train hard, win worldwide swimming championships, and go for the gold in the next Olympics.

But while celebrating a successful swim meet at his hotel bar, he meets a mysterious woman named Laila.

Not only is Laila beautiful, but she's smart, witty, and charming. So when she brazenly invites herself up to his room, he jumps at the opportunity to spend the night with her.

He gets far more than he bargained for when she bites his neck and abducts him to the hidden vampire kingdom of the Vale, changing his life forever.

If he can even call it a *life* anymore…

CLICK HERE or visit michellemadow.com/freevampirerules to grab The Vampire Rules and start reading now.

ABOUT THE AUTHOR

Michelle Madow is a USA Today bestselling author of fast paced fantasy novels that will leave you turning the pages wanting more! Her books are full of magic, adventure, romance, and twists you'll never see coming.

Click here or visit author.to/MichelleMadow to view a full list of Michelle's novels on Amazon.

To get free books, exclusive content, and instant updates from Michelle, visit www.michellemadow.com/subscribe and subscribe to her newsletter now!

THE ANGEL GIFT

Published by Dreamscape Publishing

Copyright © 2018 Michelle Madow

ISBN: 9781720232513

❀ Created with Vellum

Made in the USA
Middletown, DE
12 April 2019